D0843119

What to Wear to See the Pope

MONTCLAIR HIGH SCHOOL LIBRARY
MONTCLAIR, NEW JERSEY

What to Wear to See the Pope

Christine Lehner

CARROLL & GRAF PUBLISHERS
NEW YORK

SC
LEH

WHAT TO WEAR TO SEE THE POPE

Carroll & Graf Publishers
An Imprint of Avalon Publishing Group Inc.
245 West 17th Street
New York, NY 10011

Copyright © 2004 by Christine Lehner

First Carroll & Graf edition 2004

Some of the stories in this book have appeared, in different form, in the
following publications: "Twins, Again" in *Image;* "Why the French?" in *The North
American Review;* "The Merits of Bats" in *Image;* "Lost in the Mail" in
Southwest Review.

All rights reserved. No part of this book may be reproduced in whole or in
part without written permission from the publisher, except by reviewers who
may quote brief excerpts in connection with a review in a newspaper,
magazine, or electronic publication; nor may any part of this book be
reproduced, stored in a retrieval system, or transmitted in any form or by any
means electronic, mechanical, photocopying, recording, or other, without
written permission from the publisher.

All of the characters in this book are fictitious, and any resemblance to
actual persons, living or dead, is purely coincidental.

Library of Congress Cataloging-in-Publication Data is available.

ISBN: 0-7867-1329-1

Printed in the United States of America
Interior design by Paul Paddock
Distributed by Publishers Group West

98 4573

CONTENTS

This book is for my parents, Monique and Philip Lehner

And in loving memory of
Reine Marie Garat Molkau Brancart

Twins, Again

I had always wanted to have a twin—even before Catholic school—so the results of the laparoscopy did not surprise me as much they did the others: my family, my friends, strangers on trains. Perhaps I should rephrase: I would have liked to be one of a pair of twins.

Mary and Pegeen O'Kelly were twins in a family of eleven, and for six years they were my most envied classmates at St. Agatha's. I first attempted to be friends with Pegeen, but in the end only Mary would have me. Which was not what I really would have liked: what I *wanted* was to be inside one of them, to have an *other* who knows the best and worst of you, and still has to like you. One or the other of the O'Kelly twins was usually chosen to be the Queen of May in our annual May procession honoring the Blessed Virgin. We all wore pastel dresses and had flowers in our hair, but *they* carried bouquets and were carried aloft, and no one doubted their aptness for the role.

They were not identical twins, and as such were not perfect: Pegeen O'Kelly was larger than Mary. But they were both very cute, All-American cute—they were freckled and had curly strawberry blond hair, they were stylishly chubby and wore matching smocked dresses with puffed sleeves. Later, Pegeen grew large and powerful, and might have become one of those Boadiceas on the battlefield of field hockey, had her provenance been Scotland—where such terrors proliferated—rather than Ireland. Mary grew at the generally approved rate, and developed all the generally approved protrusions. I knew I was an outsider because I was neither a twin nor Irish; but in retrospect I can see that there were plenty of other good reasons for my isolation. Mary and Pegeen did not have pale blue glasses that attenuated with pathetic menace just above their eyebrows; nor did they have legs like bleached pipe cleaners; no one would ever have referred to them as *Carpenter's dreams;* and their mother did not speak with a French accent or wear French bikinis at the yacht club.

Now, when I recall the O'Kelly twins, it seems I knew them not at all, that they were vessels for my fantasies of an *other.* I had assumed that if I had a twin, she could know the unspeakable things about me, the things I could not utter for fear the earth beneath me would groan and crack open and swallow me up. My twin, however, would naturally know these awful things and therefore, by definition, these horrors could not be ineffable. For I have come to assume that if all the prurient images and raunchy memories and sordid fantasies that clutter my brain were dragged into the light of day, then I would be a mentally healthier individual, a model of openness, untroubled by nightmares, unafraid of the confessional. Just that: daylight and utterance.

Because of the dearth of novices and younger teaching nuns, most of the Sisters of St. Joseph at our school were ancient. In their multilayered habits of black and more black, they shuffled through the halls like lost hippopotami struggling to emerge from funereal laundry piles. They were always hungry, and always forgetting where they had stashed their secret foods. In the farthest reaches of Sister Jerome's desk drawer could often be found a rotting banana, and Hostess cupcakes, and all the insects that had come to attend upon them. They ruled our little parochial school like insecure despots: arbitrarily, illogically, imagistically. (Years later in Istanbul, when I heard the story of the slightly demented Sultan Mehmed II, who sat upon his upholstered window seat in a tower of his seraglio in the Topkapi Palace, and shot at passersby for target practice, thereby proving to himself, again and again, that he was all-powerful and not to be contradicted—when I heard that story I suddenly remembered Sister Jerome, who of course didn't shoot anyone, but in her eighties had that same perverse need for reassurance that in her dementia lay her power.)

Fourth grade in parochial school was a watershed year for me. It was the year of Sister Jerome and the year I learned the exact location of our immortal souls. It was also the year I abandoned my ambition to achieve sainthood through becoming a nun. It was the beginning of the abandonment of saintly ambitions altogether, but I didn't realize that yet. My researches up to that time had been primarily in *The Saints and Your Name*, an inspirational book for children describing the lives and often gruesome deaths of the saints for whom they'd been named. The book described sixty-six saints, of whom twenty-eight were women, and of those twenty-eight women, eleven were martyred. The clear advantage of martyrdom was the instant sainthood it conferred upon the martyred; but the Emperor Diocletian and his cohorts were no longer feeding Christians to wild beasts, and besides, I was squeamish about pain. More so back then than now, but that's another matter. In later years I consulted the red-spined condensed version of Butler's *Lives of the Saints*, which listed exactly three hundred and sixty-five saints, one for each feast day of the year, and came up with fifty-three virgins and fifteen widows and only four female saints who were neither widows nor virgins. Of course, Butler was not exhaustive: he's very reticent about unverified or undocumented legends of martyrdom. For instance, he doesn't even include St. Ursula and her eleven thousand maidens, all gloriously martyred by the Huns on account of their adamant Christianity and virginity. In Attwater's compendium, a full third of the listed female saints are martyrs, and there is also a good proportion of mystics and visionaries. Anybody who knew the story of Bernadette of Lourdes, which was so popular at my school, had to at least consider the possibility of visions.

Still, in my most careful reading of the fourth grade, it became clear that there were really only two routes by which a girl achieved sainthood. She either stayed a virgin, did holy works, had visions and died young (or perhaps was cruelly martyred trying to keep her maidenhead); or else she married, was widowed, and went on to her true task in life: founding a holy order, such as the Daughters of the Cross, or The Handmaids of Mary, or the Discalced Carmelites, or the Congregation of Our Lady of the Retreat in the Cenacle, or the Society of the Little House of Divine Providence, or the Company of Mary and the Daughters of Wisdom. To confuse the issue, there was always my favorite, Joan of Arc, who—though she technically qualifies as a virgin-martyr—was an exception in that she got to dress as a man, go to war, and make a nuisance of herself to both the court and the clergy. But she is the exception that proves the rule. Sainthood appeared farther and farther beyond my reach.

Among the many misdemeanors (known to us as venial sins) available to us in our classroom were gum swallowing and hair sucking. One particularly egregious sinner was a chubby girl named Kathleen Halloran. One day, on the occasion of chastising Kathleen yet again for chewing on her long brown braid in class, Sister Jerome undertook to illustrate for us why this habit was so pernicious. She drew an extremely vague outline of a sexless human body. More or less where the uterus is located in the female (although I was clueless about anatomy at the time and am only marginally better now) she drew a circle (or an approximation of a circle: Sister Jerome was no Giotto), and she proceeded to decorate the circumference with blobs at fairly regular intervals. Then, more or less between the blobs she drew tiny lines that extended about a quarter of the way into the center of the circle—they were slightly wavy and undulated like cilia. We watched in silence as she drew. Some of us—

myself among them, it must be admitted—copied down in our notebooks whatever Sister Jerome created on the blackboard, because it was much easier to keep our mouths quiet if one or more of our extremities could be engaged. I didn't question then, nor do I doubt now, that Idle Hands really are the Devil's Work.

We waited to be told the meaning of these shapes, which represented the apex of Sister Jerome's artistic abilities. But there was more to come. Next to the larger and now decorated circle, she drew a smaller fig-like shape. A startled silence settled over the classroom like the smell of rotting fruit—for once she did not press the chalk heavily on the board, for once there were no squeaks or raspings; she drew as lightly as was possible to draw and still make a mark. Then she told us. The larger circle was a stomach, and the blobs were chewing gum and the cilia were pieces of hair, and her point was that once ingested the gum and hair remained forever affixed to the stomach lining, and, as we could imagine, the more gum and hair ingested, the less room there would be for food. That was one problem, but a far greater one was that the Host—which we all knew was the Body of Christ—also had to visit the stomach, and it would be sacrilegious for the Host to ever touch chewing gum or hair. How could we question that? Wasn't it the most painfully obvious thing we'd seen all day?

The smaller fig-like shape, she explained, was our immortal soul, and she had drawn it with a light touch because, as we knew, when the life had long gone from our earthbound bodies and they were buried in consecrated ground awaiting the Last Judgment, our immortal souls would be hanging out in Hell, Purgatory—the most likely, or Heaven. (Limbo, at any rate, was not a possibility for us, because we were all baptized Catholics.) To further elucidate, Sister Jerome made small dots all around the soul, and declared them to be our venial sins; and then, to our great dismay, she turned the chalk sideways to the blackboard, and smudged certain largish dark spots inside the soul: these were our mortal sins, the absolution for which was stringent and essential, if we wanted to avoid the flames of Hell.

She did not explain the relationship between the misplaced stomach and the soul, and so we were left to assume it was the obvious one: proximity.

Thirty-odd years after the fourth grade, I was home one evening with my husband and children; we were eating pasta for dinner. In my daughter's nutritional pyramid, pasta occupies all levels: Winnie does not like the sun to set on a day without pasta. That evening I had in fact planned a more varied meal and had poached some shad. But upon tasting it I detected an overstrong metallic flavor, a whiff of sulfur. In a panic I removed all the fish from my family's plates and wrapped it in tinfoil—to mask the odor and thus protect Felix, the neighbor's cat, from his own greed and gluttony, although I don't know why, since I loathed the slinking, smug self-satisfied creature who often taunted my precious bulldog, who of course could not climb trees—and put it all in a garbage bag, which I took outside and placed securely inside the garbage can under the back porch. I have a not entirely irrational fear of poisoning my family with my culinary mistakes; and who knows what nuclear waste was being spewed into the river just as that particular shad was having its dinner. There is always with me the memory of the summer when the horseshoe crabs died en masse and backfloated all over Headsup Bay. I knew very well just how ancient and resilient the horseshoe crabs were. Hadn't I been brought up knowing how they cohabited the earth with dinosaurs (now mercifully extinct), and how *Limulus polyphemus* remained: unchanged, unrepentant? That was the summer before Plymouth Two was forced to shut down because it had been releasing its circulating coolant water into the Bay. That was all, just warm water, they said.

It was a Friday evening, and it had been a long time since the Church demanded of the faithful fish on Fridays; but no matter, sometimes towards the end of the week, something would swim up inside me, and I would crave that flaky smelly pelagic-flesh, the sour lingering taste of Galilee. It seems very unlikely that the craving for fish had anything to do with the bizarre medical tests I had undergone that morning, painless but still bizarre, and from which I expected to learn nothing that I didn't already know: which was that I was unable to get pregnant again and that there was no organic reason that any doctor would acknowledge—which allowed them to describe my complaint as idiopathic, which characterization I tried not to take personally—although they might hint that a botched emergency appendectomy performed on April Fools' Day a few years earlier might, just might, have spewed out some flotsam and created anatomical obstacles.

But the panic over a possible poisoning banished all desire for fish, and pasta was the comfort food of choice. When the phone rang, we were arguing about the meaning of *apocryphal*. For a merely semantic argument, it was beginning to turn nasty. I was telling, or more likely retelling, a story about the time my grandmother took me to Belgium when I was twelve and I learned of her first, and passionate, and doomed marriage. And my husband referred to something in the story as apocryphal. Until very recently in my life, I had misused the word *apocryphal* (which I now know means of questionable authorship or authenticity, or erroneous or fictitious—from the Apocrypha in the Bible). I had confused it with *apocalyptic* (which, by contrast, means great or total devastation, or doom, or a prophetic disclosure, or a revelation—this also, and not surprisingly, from the Apocalypse foretold in the Book of Revelations). I had done this with other words, such as tepid and torpid, or what is worse, delinquent and deliquesce, making more or less an ass of myself on occasion, depending on how desperately I wanted to seem intelligent. But that evening I knew most definitely what apocryphal meant, because, having made an especial ass of myself in a certain situation to remain unnamed, I had looked it up and impressed it upon my right brain, and thus I realized that I was being accused of a falsehood, a prevarication, at best hyperbole. I asked my husband if he knew what *apocryphal* meant, and if that was what he meant to say.

And he answered Yes, of course, he knew what it meant, and he had said just what he meant.

Then I asked So what does *apocryphal* mean? Because I was

pretty sure he was making the same perfectly understandable error I had made all those years, but he balked at being
asked for a definition. And I got quite huffy and implied he
didn't know what he was saying, and he got huffier, and
indignant that I should ask him to define terms, and so on.
Then Cosmo, my son, produced the OED, of which we have
all thirteen volumes ranged on a nearby shelf in the pantry,
because of just this sort of inevitable prandial conflict. The
definition therein mollified us both. Yet, being perilously
insistent and veering toward a justification that could only
bring misery upon us both, I pointed out that my definition
(*of doubtful authenticity, spurious*) was listed first, while his (*mythical*) was last. By that point, the argument no longer had
anything to do with semantics (if it had ever) and was clearly
yet another version of our marital discord and our mutually
exclusive needs to own the authorized version of life as we
lived it. As such, it was an exceptionally silly thing to argue
about—or was it? It was perhaps not entirely a red herring—
and we might have come to blows, or at least hurled dictionaries, and further damaged our children's psyches and
any hopes they had for emotional well-being in later life,
had the phone not rung.

With immense relief to be rescued from her parents'
bathetic need to win arguments, my daughter answered the
phone. She was silent—in such a way that we knew it wasn't
for her—and then she said, "It's someone with an accent for
you, Mom." I had no idea who it was, but I was sure that
whoever it was had heard her comment, and I wasn't
pleased. And since when were accents something we com-

mented upon in this house? I took the phone and went as far from the kitchen as the twenty-five-foot cord would allow. It's the longest curlicue cord you can buy at our hardware store, and it's what I have installed on all our telephones.

Dr. von Pfefferlingel was on the phone, and he indeed has an accent, as he is from Heidelberg, and I am immensely fond of his accent. He didn't seem to have noticed Winnie's comment. I was not displeased to hear from him, mostly because of the accent, which was the trait I sought out most consciously in doctors. Because of it, he had become for me a fusion of my beloved grandmother, my Chilean psychiatrist with one leg, Goethe, Hildegard von Bingen, and my gynecologist, which he was. But just then he went so quickly into what I think of as his Reassuring Mode that I became a bit anxious. Not overly anxious, because back then I still believed he could fix whatever might ail me, although there didn't seem to be anything that did. So, after quelling my admiration for his accent, I heard him say that there were tumors attached to my ovaries and they needed to be removed. Soon.

No matter what the topic, this conversation would have been difficult on account of the susurration in the kitchen and the lingering animosity of *apocryphal*, but Dr. von Pfefferlingel is remarkably kind and so repeated very slowly for me a diagnosis that sounded mythical, perhaps even apocalyptic. In my uterus were two dermoid tumors known as *teratomas*. A teratoma is a teratoid tumor, teratoid meaning *Having the appearance or character of a monster or monstrous formation*. It comes from *terat*, the Greek for monster, or marvel. Of course at the time I didn't know this etymology (which study I had frequently confused with entomology—the fascination with creepy-crawlies). All I heard was that there were two of these large growths, growing inside me; one was characterized as larger than grapefruit but smaller than a watermelon. It is my limited experience that doctors analogize the size of any mass to citrus fruit. At some point I must have said something vaguely alarming, because the chatter in the kitchen abruptly ceased and my family began to listen, mostly to my silence. *Herr Doktor* explained that teratomas were congenital tumors due to inclusion in one fetus or another. What? That the cells had been there all along, that the cells from which these things grew were there when I was born, and before, when I free-floated inside my mother. What the doctor told me was that these tumors usually contain tissue from other parts of the body, tissue that might have been part of another fetus altogether: hair, teeth, bones, or skin. I was having a bit of trouble understanding the medical terminology—but no trouble at all visualizing the tumor—and it looked remarkably like my immortal soul besmirched with a lifetime of unconfessed sins.

Two days later I was dressed in a dingy blue johnny; as instructed, it was tied to open in the front—this was not much of a concession to my modesty. And although it seemed to me I was perfectly capable of walking, I was wheeled into the Operating Theater. My glasses had earlier been removed for my own safety, so the bile-green walls and metallic instruments diabolically blurred into a vision of a spring morning tinged with frigid dew, and potent with death. Even without my glasses, I could tell that the doctors and nurses were all masked. On wheels, I was pushed through the door of the Operating Theater. Two voices from within called out "Not yet. We're still mopping up in here. The last one was difficult." I was wheeled backwards into the sickly green hallway.

"Mopping up?" I asked no one in particular—because without my glasses it was hard to make eye contact, or any contact whatever. "What are they mopping up?"

Then Dr. von Pfefferlingel came along and we spoke and I felt completely safe. Before counting backwards for the anesthesiologist, I replied to someone that No, I wasn't particularly scared.

The surgery didn't take the scheduled one hour. For five hours I never knew were passing, that disappeared from my life, Dr. von Pfefferlingel scraped away at my inner organs. (Later, his wife told me—in German—that he had such remarkable stamina because he lifted weights every day after office hours, no matter how late it was. "He can do what is generally considered impossible, or not worth the trouble," she told me. I envied them their mutual admiration.)

The next day—I think it was the next day when they were kind enough to remove the tubes from my nose and throat, and give me more than an ice cube to suck on; and while I was still in an extremely pleasant morphine fog, and certainly that was the way I wanted to stay, given the alternative—Dr. von Pfefferlingel came, as ever a vision of Teutonic elegance in his dark blue suit, and sat on the end of my hospital bed. After delicately picking his way through the scar tissue from the botched appendectomy of April Fools', he said, he had found and removed the offending teratomas.

"The size of melons," he told me, ratcheting the size up the fruit-scale. We had left the citrus analogies behind.

"May I see them?" I asked.

Sorry, they'd already gone down to pathology.

Well, then, what did they look like?

"Just gloppy melon-sized masses filled with blond hair," he told me.

"Blond hair?" I repeated, somewhat idiotically, because the morphine was remarkably good at altering perceptions as well as pain.

"Blond hair," he repeated. He said he'd never actually seen one with hair before; teeth were slightly more the norm as teratomal inclusions. At this point I became acutely aware of my own post-op disarray, the unwashed scraggly quasi-blond hair, the wrinkled hospital johnny, the pool of blood in which I seemed to generally recline, and, of course, the industrial-strength staples that bisected my abdomen. I did not feel at all lovely or even barely decent, and Dr. von Pfefferlingel was so well-groomed and charming that I felt ashamed for not having made a greater effort, or any effort at all. Instead of which I lay there, pale and sanguineous, impatient for the next morphine shot.

"Just how did it get there?" I whispered, because I wasn't sure I wanted to hear the answer, and I hoped he would whisper in reply.

"Ah," he said. "The cells were always there, from the time

you were a fetus. They're quite rare, and as to what causes them to start growing, we really don't know."

"Could I have . . . ?"

"No, there's nothing you could have done to make them grow. Or stop them, for that matter."

"Well, where did the hair come from? Could that hair have been for a twin?"

"Oh not really, since it comes from undifferentiated cells, but it is the sort of anomaly that leads to headlines in the *National Enquirer* like . . . oh, like WOMAN SHOCKS DOCS— LOOKING FOR APPENDIX THEY FIND HER FORTY-YEAR-OLD BLOND TWIN."

"You're kidding?" I said.

"*Naturlich.* I don't really read those papers, but I see the headlines. They can make anything sound outrageous—but see, here you are, and it's not so amazing."

I had to think about that: Why not so amazing?

I said, "How about . . . SIBLING RIVALRY IN THE WOMB LEADS TO MIDDLE AGED OVARIAN HAIRBALL, or . . . TWIN SISTERS IN THE WOMB—ONLY ONE IS BORN—THE OTHER DISCOVERED FORTY YEARS LATER WHEN HER TWIN'S APPENDIX BURSTS; SHE'S STILL A BLONDE WHILE HER OLDER TWIN GOES TO BEAUTY SALON ONCE A MONTH; or . . . "

We laughed, but of course it's not particularly comfortable to laugh when there are needles sticking out of your arms and staples marching up your middle. So I made one of those proper smirks that made me think of headmistresses, and then it wasn't very funny anymore.

Sharing the room with me was an older woman who

spent her entire time on the telephone with her parish priest and a certain Sister Felicity; with the priest she tended to be unctuous and grateful for all his prayers, such as they were; with Sister Felicity she rhapsodized about her symptoms, and in particular she enumerated every bowel movement she'd had since entering the hospital three weeks earlier. And there were many. And every effort was counted as well. When my sister came to visit we had to cover our mouths with pillows, we thought it was so funny; Sophie's bloodstream was not flowing with morphine, and she also thought it was funny, which I found reassuring. We were remembering the time a much younger Cosmo had meningitis in Costa Rica, and of course we were terrified because we were up in the coffee-growing mountains quite far from what is commonly referred to as modern medicine. But at the same time we didn't know enough to be all that terrified. Cosmo, who was in terrible pain and unnervingly bluish, kept track of every time he threw up. So every single time he dribbled out some pathetic amount of vomit, he would say weakly *That's the seventh*, or *eighth time, just in one day*, and he might add *Have you ever thrown up so much?* And all this not without a certain amount of pride. He has always been a child who enjoys quantitative information, statistics, and, especially, world records.

Daily, I was bleeding less and less, and the staples were beginning to itch. One day after my sheets were changed I found this list written on the new sheets, obviously in indelible ink:

1. GORK
2. Bad Outcome
3. Gastronomy
4. Go Home with P-Barb
5. See Joanie
6. Sleeze Ball
7. No She can't have cabfare to Yonkers

I spent a lot of time reading and memorizing that list, because I knew that sooner or later my sheets would be changed again, and it would be gone. The night nurse explained that Gork meant brain damage, that it was not really slang, but quite technical. Everyone in the hospital referred to a certain loss of brain functions that way. I was grateful for the definition.

Pathology, apparently, quite greedily uses up all one's tumors so there is nothing left to bring home for the mantel or the vitrine. Thus I went home empty-handed, unless one counts the staples—which I did, and there were sixteen.

Weeks later I fell into a deep depression. It was as if I'd moved into a house that had only sharp angles, and there wasn't a single place to sit or lie down comfortably, and the only things to read were instruction manuals for appliances, and the lightbulbs were never stronger than 25 watts. I was bereft, because I knew that there had been a twin, and I had lost her somewhere along the way. I was mourning her.

A long time ago, in another life perhaps, I wrote and published a story called "Twins." It was about female identical twins, whose parents die and leave them moderately well-off but clueless. One of them marries a man called Victor, who clearly is in love with both twins; the other attempts suicide five times, and writes a series of notes which are increasingly less arch, and the last one is true enough to explain away her life; so she succeeds in dying. It's very sad, of course, but there's also a lot of funny stuff, about garden tools, and sex, and topiary figures on the lawn, and lecherous young uncles, and marriage, and marsupials. But when I reread it, all I see is how much I wanted a twin, any twin. I was having more and more trouble being just me.

I had many fantasies about Dr. von Pfefferlingel, this voyeur of my innards; most of them involved his presence and assistance as I bravely gave birth to twins, twins who emerged already fluent in their private language.

In a book called *Curious Tales of Twins*, which Dr. von Pfefferlingel would surely not have read because there is nothing at all scientific about it, and in fact it is somewhat akin to a hardcover *National Enquirer*, I found this under the heading "Twin Abnormalities":

> *"Still rarer than these circumstances, fortunately, are the occasions when a twin lies dormant within a body for many years, undiscovered, and then has to be surgically removed. These growths are called teratomas and in ancient times were prized for divination. At least some authorities speculate that teratomas are twins; others consider them tumors derived from germ cells."*

I didn't like the use of the word "fortunately" in the first sentence; I took it rather personally, and so I did not show this book to anyone.

Then one day, while browsing through the eleventh edition of *French's Index of Differential Diagnosis*, that delightful compendium of disease and abnormality, which boasts no less than two hundred and eighty color illustrations, I found something else quite remarkable. For me, it was almost a gift, and almost a booby prize.

> *"At the turn of this century a hair ball or trichobezoar was frequently encountered as an epigastric mass in hysterical girls who chewed and swallowed their hair, which then formed as an exact mould of the stomach. Hairballs are only rarely encountered in these days and modern textbooks hardly mention them; however as fashions and hair styles change they may reappear on the clinical scene."*

These two sentences out of thousands were graced with not one, but two color photographs, in which the hairball looked to me more like a meteor or volcanic rock. I wanted to send a copy to Sister Jerome at Saint Blandina's Home for Retired Nuns, but she had been dead for decades. I thought and thought about sending a copy to Dr. von Pfefferlingel, accompanied by some witty comment by myself, but in the end I never did.

It was clear that I was hopelessly and pointlessly in love with my doctor. I realized that, there on his feet for hours in the Operating Theater, he had surely seen my immortal soul—wasn't it right there, a fig-like and ethereal shape amidst the organs and tubes and flotsam and *teratomas?*—he had seen it and he had not rejected me out of hand. The very next day, and the next day and the next, he had sat on my bed and talked to me, all in his lovely accent, as if I were a perfectly normal person.

Still Saigon

I t is pleasant to imagine how they look: my elderly parents in airports. Colette, my diminutive mother, smoothes her pale silver hair, which is pulled back into a mysterious chignon. It is mysterious to me because I have never been able to replicate it. It does not matter how many times I have seen her slender fingers gravitate to the back of her head, engage in a flurry of activity, and then return to stillness, while a folded construction of layered tresses is revealed, worthy of an origami master. She wears one of her countless interchangeable French suits in every permutation of purple and mauve and fuchsia and royal blue, each one with embossed gold or brass buttons that hint of Roman coinage or French military honors. It is only the physical stature of my parents that diminishes with age; their emotional presence looms hugely for all of us.

Standing beside her is my father, Daniel, whenever possible on the telephone, in his gray flannels and blue jacket, in every country in every climate. His snow-white hair is so meticulously combed that the teeth marks are visible. This would not be remarkable were it not for his eyebrows: vast and unruly, long, curling, and bushy. They are chaotic snowdrifts. They are exploding eiderdown pillows. They hover perilously over his eyes and then dart upwards like fluffy egrets.

It used to be that our parents could be found standing side by side among the telephones mounted on walls, or sitting in adjoining carrels in airline lounges, calling their five grown children. Now they have their cellular phones, with special attachments for the hearing-impaired; but the program is the same. As they circumnavigate the globe and revisit world capitals and the ruins of lost cities, they have designated the downtime between flights to catch up on family gossip: to impart decorating and fashion advice (my mother with her daughters) and to talk monthly sales figures (my father with James and Olivier) or the coffee futures market (with Gabriel), or simply to find out how many grandchildren they now have. They are systematic. They always start with the eldest, me, Ursula, and then go on to James, Gabriel, Sophie, and Olivier. It has to be a life-or-death matter for one of them to depart from this formula, largely because at this point the foreordained order is established and we have accepted our ordinal place. Perhaps it is easy for me to say that, about acceptance, since I am the eldest and therefore first to be called. (That is my assumption.) Perhaps that is why they settled on that system in the first place, rather than alphabetical (which would make me last) or reverse chronological (which would make me last again), or chronologically by our birthdays (which would make me third), because they know I tend to be extremely sensitive to slights, imagined slights, injustices, and the whole psychological compendium of dysfunctional parent-child relations.

Of course my siblings and I have never bothered to ascertain for sure whether or not they really call us in order. Given that at least three times out of five they are answered with a machine, it would be rather difficult. At times, I think, they are just as grateful for the machine, for the ritual politeness, for the obligatory listing of the house's inhabitants (which in the case of my siblings who have more children than I do—four, five, and four—always seems a tad proud, even boastful; perhaps I am slightly neurotic about this, so I have determined to say nothing, a novel pursuit), and also for the instructions. Some of us leave more explicit instructions than others. One brother's machine instructs the caller to leave a message in short, clearly enunciated sentences, amounting to no more than four minutes, and under no circumstances to neglect to include the date and time of the call. Another brother's voice mendaciously announces that all of them, and he lists them all, all four children, are out for just a second and someone will call back in just a second, which they never do; my brother-in-law once gave updates on the progress of my baby sister's labor: for example, twelve hours and two centimeters dilated. Another machine (mine) suggests that you may, if you so desire, leave a message for Saint Joan, who is my bulldog. Most of my siblings think this is idiotic; they also think my dog is very ugly, which may account for their weird prejudice.

So, on her way back from a trip to Vietnam and Cambodia, my mother called from the San Francisco airport, and I was actually home and answering the phone. She told me she had been to see deux cent seize rue Pelerin, the house in Saigon where she had lived as a child, over fifty years ago.

It was eerie to be hearing that from her, because almost everything I know about that house, and their brief time in Indochina, I know from my grandmother, and it is largely about loss.

"How did you find it, did you still know your way around?"

"Not exactly," she said. "The guide was able to help but the main thing was that it was one of only two streets which still retained their French names. Even though it's not the same French name, not rue Pelerin, anymore. Now it's rue Pasteur because Pasteur is about the only Frenchman the Vietnamese don't hate, since he and a colleague came up with a cure for some nasty virus in the Mekong. And the other street was rue Catinat, where your grandmother loved to shop."

"So you found the house?"

"Oh well, you could hardly see the façade because of all the little shops. The whole street is commercial now. The big tree in front is gone. Everything is changed."

I asked my mother "So what was it like?" I was looking for something very specific, some architectural detail or anomaly of the flora and fauna that would illuminate her brief life there, and thus, by association or genetics, help me to explain my personal pathology. I have this thing about secrets in my family. There are the secrets that are truly kept hidden, which of course I will do my best to unearth. And there are the secrets by default, kept because no one has yet managed to ask the right questions. So I keep asking, and looking for the clue, the Rosetta stone to my family. It might be argued that here is a clear case of a woman who needs something more useful to keep her occupied. Why, for instance, do I need to know why my father's mother received electroshock therapy, repeatedly? How will this knowledge get me any closer to the resolution I long for?

"Do you remember *Doctor Zhivago*?" my mother asked me. She was ever fond of the Socratic method.

"Yes," I said, although I could not recite it, chapter and verse, as my mother could; nor could I work up a similar passion for Omar Sharif. But I said "Yes" right away, because generally the reference becomes clear with the context. So I said "Yes."

"Well, it was just like that. Except that *Doctor Zhivago* was the sanitized version. In our house there were families living in every one of the rooms. There was a whole family in my bedroom, and another one in Pierre's and all the moldings had been torn down and all the doors were gone, and every door was solid steel and had at least three or four locks."

"They actually let you in?"

"Well, we got into the house, but people were not friendly. No, not at all. The guide said not to mention we'd owned the house, to just say we'd rented it and lived there a while. There was a room on the second floor that had been Mother's sitting room and now it had a big steel door—the kind you might have in a bank, or a meat locker—and it had a little window in it, but covered with a steel panel and a grill, and so our guide knocked and knocked and asked if we might come in, but the old woman who answered, well, first she wouldn't answer, and then she refused to speak French, but finally she said she couldn't let us in because, she said, every morning when her husband and son went off to work they locked her in and took away the key."

They locked her in, one tiny Vietnamese woman passing her days in a small room where more than fifty years ago Bonne Maman sat in the evenings and embroidered flowers and knit sweaters for another climate. Could this be the clue I was looking for? What language must I speak in order to learn something from this old woman? Could she communicate with my grandmother, my beloved Bonne Maman, who is well into the last stages of Alzheimer's, and speaks completely genteel nonsense in two languages but still enjoys oysters and champagne?

And still, sometimes Bonne Maman can fool you. She will utter a phrase so ordinary and logical that you think she means it just as you understand it, and you respond, and then discover how wrong you are. Once, when Cosmo was in the room, she said "What a nice young man," and I smiled and said that yes, he was very nice. And then she said, in French, that she had not killed the rabbits.

"Was it awful?" I asked my mother, because I still dream almost every night of the landscape and architecture and rooms of the old house we lived in until I was twelve, when my grandfather died and we moved to his house. I have never been back to that old house, with its darknesses, and slanting roof, and corridors leading nowhere, with its terrors, although I often drive by it; it is a house of dreams and without it I fear I would be homeless or a nomad in my dreams.

I asked my mother, "Did anything look the same?"

"You cannot imagine how different it was, and still standing. In the front hall there were black and white marble tiles, which were lovely for roller-skating, and I could still see some tiles in patches, but that was all. In the yard where Pierre played, and out back where the kitchen was, and then the houses for the servants, there were two new rows of houses, or really just apartments. Probably a hundred people lived there."

"But I can imagine," I said. I hate to be told there is anything I cannot imagine.

That evening I told my husband that Mom had called from the airport, which was nothing new, and that she had seen her old house in Saigon.

"I think it's called Ho Chi Minh City now," Gus pointed out. He is the type of person who called Burma Myanmar within twenty-four hours of the name change, while I tend toward a modern amnesia and will even affectedly refer to Constantinople. I always used to confuse the German Federal Republic and the German Democratic Republic, so was grateful on many levels when they reunited. Gus also calls Cambodia Kampuchea, and I am not proud to admit how much this annoys me.

"Do you remember *Doctor Zhivago*?" I asked him. "The scene where Zhivago and Geraldine Chaplin come back to their house in Moscow after the Revolution, and there are dozens of families living there in their old rooms and they feel so terribly unwelcome. That's what it was like."

"That just shows how oppressive they were," he said.

"Who is *they*?" I asked, although I knew, and I knew where we were heading.

"The French imperialists. They. Looting and raping the sacred sites and imposing monoculture on the peasants."

"Oh, *they*. You mean my grandparents, and the rubber planters, the oil merchants, the jade collectors, the mah-jongg French ladies, the opium-smoking fornicators, the sisters of the Convent of the Birds, the aphrodisiac smugglers, and the Jesuits, and my grandparents."

"Don't get hyper," he said. "It doesn't suit you. Would you rather I said the American military-industrial complex? I didn't say it was your mother's fault."

He is wrong, of course. It does suit me. And he didn't need to say it was Mother's fault, or my fault. I didn't need to hear it to know what it meant.

Of all the places my mother lived as a child, she was in Indochina the shortest time. And of that time, she was mostly in the Couvent des Oiseaux, up in Dalat, in the mountains where it is cooler and the air more salubrious. Years earlier, French nuns had founded the school at the behest of the Empress of Cochinchine, who, before her arranged marriage to the Emperor, had been educated at the

Couvent des Oiseaux in Paris. She had loved it so much she wanted to re-create that cloistered serenity in her own tropical land, but as far from the malarial lowlands as possible. According to Bonne Maman, the girls there had the loveliest uniforms, beige linen jumpers with white blouses, and each class had a different colored polka-dot ribbon to tie in bows round their necks. My mother's ribbon was blue and white and so she asked her mother to knit her a little sweater to match, which of course Bonne Maman did, knitting in the infernal humidity of Saigon, while imagining the breezes in the Dalat mountains, breezes that actually moved the oversized leaves of mountain rhododendrons, breezes that could actually chill a small girl and raise the pale downy hairs of her arms. But when Bonne Maman visited her daughter awhile later, the sweater was gone. When she asked, my mother told her it had been eaten by a tiger. Of course this was impossible. The convent was surrounded by a high stone wall, and guarded by huge wrought-iron gates. The girls inside were as safe as could be.

Then in 1939 the Germans invaded Belgium and the Japanese came sweeping south through China. By 1940, the French had surrendered in Europe and could spare no energies or resources for a colony on the other side of the globe. In September 1940, the Japanese demanded of the Vichy government that they be allowed to station troops in Tonkin, and on September 22 they were in occupation. Meanwhile, with the war in Europe there were no goods being delivered to the colonials, no Evian water, no French wine. At the beginning, the Europeans had enough supplies in storage;

but then, bit by bit, things started changing. There was an order from all the embassies that European and American women must wear their shorts at least one inch below the knee, as the shorter shorts offended the Japanese sense of modesty. Then at the club, because Japanese officers were coming there, women were no longer allowed to wear revealing bathing suits—which for the French are a national and inalienable right, like garlic or good wine.

It happened quickly and yet imperceptibly; one month they were living in the most beautiful outpost of the French empire, in huge airy colonnaded houses whose sultry gardens burst with odoriferous almost nauseating erotic blossoms, attending nightly cocktail parties, dining at the club, shopping on rue Catinat. They were eating the Chinese cuisine, which everyone agreed was the only cuisine in the world as complex and delicious as the French. They were wearing dresses of exquisite Chinese silks fastened by tiny frogs in matching silk, made by Chinese dressmakers trained by Parisian couturiers. If they read the papers, they knew that the Japanese were moving south through China; but that was so far away, and surely they would be stopped by the greater allied forces, quite soon. Then the next month, or so it seemed, they could not get the bottled water they needed to take their daily quinine, and they heard disquieting and finally terrifying stories of what happened to compatriots captured and put into prisoner-of-war camps by the Japanese in occupied China.

So when my mother's appendix ruptured, she went to a military hospital in Saigon. Because it was a military hospital, there were only male nurses, and Bonne Maman, considering it unseemly for her ten-year-old daughter to be cared for by strange men, stayed with her in the hospital. Thus Bonne Maman wasn't home when three days later word came from all their embassies that European and American women and children should leave Indochina, and right away, because their safety could no longer be guaranteed. They were told there would be a ship of the Messagerie Maritime ready to take them, but only to Manila, as it could not leave Indochinese waters, and that it was leaving the port of Saigon in twenty-four hours.

Two things constantly remind us of this evacuation: the size of my mother's appendix scar, which is about twelve inches long and still noticeable, not that it ever stopped her from wearing bikinis; and the fact that she and my uncle and grandmother have nothing of value that belonged to them in Indochina, no treasures, no objets, no photographs, no paintings. My grandmother told the maid to pack for the journey only clothes and toys for the children, and thus they left behind the lovely jade and ivories, the portraits of the children, the dining room chairs whose cushions she had embroidered—squinting through a magnifying glass—with the dahlias and roses of a Belgian garden, the furniture, the rugs, all the china except for two plates, and all her party dresses. I think it is the loss of the party dresses I mind the most. Bonne Maman later learned that a Japanese general had moved into their house. She always wondered what he made of the portraits of Colette and Pierre, those pale Belgian children determined not to smile for the over-eager portraitist, a young Frenchman making his living documenting the offspring of the colonials. Like a wide assortment of young men, he fell slightly in love with my grandmother. The story is that both portraits resembled Bonne Maman far more than Colette and Pierre.

With my grandmother was her friend Violet Gordon, whose husband Laurie worked with Bon Papa. When I first heard of Laurie Gordon, and even later when I met him, I thought he was a cross between Lawrence of Arabia and General George Gordon of Khartoum fame. And like Peter O'Toole, he was Scottish and extremely handsome. Violet, who seemed indistinguishable from the Queen Mother, which resemblance she cultivated, was famous for washing her face with real strawberries. She mashed strawberries all over her face, then sat happily in her dressing room and chatted. Later, with a flannel—which is what the British call washcloths, presumably because they think washcloths are related to pajamas—she wiped off the pink mush full of tiny black seeds that looked unnervingly like very tiny insects. As a result of this, she had the most beautiful complexion you could imagine. Violet and her two sons were Bonne Maman and Colette and Pierre's companions for the next four years, although none of them knew it would be thus as they left Saigon harbor in the middle of the night to wait out the brief war.

The captain of the ship that took the women and children to Manila in October of 1940 was not sympathetic to his passengers: elegant ladies and their confused children. Bonne Maman told me "The food was pitiful, because the captain, being Vichy, wanted us to live the same way they were living in France, on rations, and so they would serve nothing but herring for the children—every meal was creamed herring. Breakfast was creamed herring in a bowl. Lunch was creamed herring on a plate. Dinner was creamed herring again. I didn't know there was so much herring in the world." The mothers got together as a group and went to the captain asking for something a bit more palatable, if only for the children, porridge or something, but he did not relent. He said that was all there was.

When the French ship's doctor visited their cabin, he discovered that Colette's incision was becoming infected. But there were no medical supplies onboard. Bonne Maman said to him, "Well, doctor, I do have this bottle of good English whiskey," and he said, "Fine, we'll use it." Thus sterilized, he resewed the incision with catgut.

After four days they landed in Manila, then under American protection. An ambulance met them at the pier and took my mother to the American hospital. The French doctor went along to explain, because he was so embarrassed by the miserable state of her wound. The doctors there re-opened the incision, disinfected it, and put her back together, and that is why the scar is now almost a foot long. And yet, for all its antiquity, it is not so hideous as mine. Is this the clue I am looking for? That both my mother and I have abdominal scars inappropriate to modern medicine? Hers did not keep her from wearing bikinis; mine came later in life, and did. But then I am not a European, and that makes all the difference in the matter of bikinis. As well, my scar is not the badge of a ruptured appendix, but a dark angry slash from the belly button on down, where I was cut open on three separate occasions. And each time, it seems to me, they never found exactly what they were looking for, or hoping for, or even what they expected, but rather some visceral mess or tabloid anomaly, and I was always sorry to disappoint the charming doctors.

That group of women and children stayed in Manila for two weeks, waiting for an American ship. They stayed in what was said to have been the best hotel in Manila. It was completely round, with a round dining room and curved impractical walls. When Bonne Maman first told me of the round hotel I imagined these refugee women going from room to room, trailing their manicured fingers along the concave arcs of the inner walls, writing the names of their husbands, left behind in Indochina, on scraps of hotel stationery and stuffing the tiny folded pieces of paper into the cracks, where giant tropical earwigs and geckos lived their sultry lives. I imagined the women dancing with each other in the round ballroom, back when they still thought the war would be over in a few months and that they would return to the life they understood in Saigon or Tonkin or Dalat.

The hotel staff was on strike, and so the women and children fended for themselves, or almost, making their own beds, and serving themselves from a buffet. They were waiting for a ship. Bonne Maman told me, "Now when we were in Manila, they said there is no boat for you. There is no boat you can take. So we were all women and children, with no winter clothes, leaving and not knowing where our husbands were, going to another country—so we were, as the captain would say, a bunch of wild women and children."

Mostly they were Americans, and hoping for an American ship. But after two weeks of limbo in Manila, they were grateful for a British ship even if it was only going to Hong Kong. So they went to Hong Kong, where most of them had friends, and once again, though briefly, life took on its normal shape of sociability and privilege.

Yet Bonne Maman said this was a very sad time for them. She would say, "We were only women and children, and very depressed." When I was a very young woman, I objected very much to her saying this, because she was my beloved Bonne Maman whom I admired above all others. I wanted to hear how bravely they managed without the men, how independent they were. Knowing how much I resembled her, I wanted testimony that there was hope for my own dependent morass that always looked abroad, afield and away for validation. I would mutter, to us both, *Oh Bonne Maman, Please don't say ONLY like that. Because you are not ONLY a woman, you are my heroine. You are the Bonne Maman whose arms, even now, frail as birds wings draped with faded silk, give shape to the air pockets around me, who gives shape to my life.* And it did seem a terrible contradiction, that Bonne Maman, who was so brave and self-sufficient, would readily—in a flash, in a nanosecond—cede responsibility and power to a man. She believed firmly in the adage that it is useful to have a man around the house. She even prayed to male saints, something I will only do in specific reference to her. She adored men, and men in turn adored her. Now, this no longer seems contradictory or even undesirable.

Finally the American liner, SS *President Polk*, arrived in Hong Kong to transport the waylaid exiles to California. At that time there was a small fleet of American ocean liners, all named for different presidents. James Polk, as you may recall, became president in 1845, and it was during his tenure that we won the Mexican-American War and thus acquired California, Texas, Colorado, Utah, Arizona, New Mexico, Wyoming, and Nevada, without which, if you think about it, we would have no movie industry, no avocados, no surfing, no powder skiing, no cactus gardens, no Walt Disney, and no dude ranches. There would be no illegal immigrants in LA, and Mexico would have Olympic skiers. It seems fairly clear why the shipping company would name a liner for Polk, rather than Millard Fillmore or Grover Cleveland, for instance.

And so, from Hong Kong, Bonne Maman and her two children embarked on the third and longest leg of their journey. For reasons mysterious to Bonne Maman but presumably due to wartime exigencies, the ship sailed north of Japan. Since all the evacuees were fleeing tropical countries, they had no winter clothes. There was, however, plenty of food. My grandmother said the poor captain was going out of his mind; he said to her, "Madame Lévesque, I would prefer the whole American army to all you young and pretty girls." She said to me, "We were young, you know, and with young children." As if that explained it all.

Most of the time they traveled under blackout conditions. Not long out of Hong Kong, they hit the tail of a typhoon. Once Bonne Maman looked out her porthole and saw a wave cresting twenty meters above her. She thought, *C'est fini. That wave is going over us and it is the last of us. Poor Olivier* (my grandfather) *won't even be able to bury our bodies. Does one wear black for the drowned but never found?* (This mattered to Bonne Maman, who set out to wear black for seven years when my grandfather died, until, after two or three years, my mother and I begged her to lighten up a bit, and wear some gray and lavender, which suited her so much better. She was not built like Queen Victoria, and black always shrunk her.)

Everyone was seasick except Bonne Maman, who always had a stable stomach. Wherever she was, she found her equilibrium point. So she went from cabin to cabin looking after vomiting children and their mothers. Of course, the captain thought she was wonderful. That never surprised me. I can't imagine anyone I would rather have to comfort me, as I vomit, than Bonne Maman. I often told my children this story, part of the constant retelling of the wonders of their great-grandmother, so that they can recite most of her adventures by heart. This is especially important now that she no longer knows the difference between *aimer* and *amer*, between Indochina and Alexandria, between the Flemish and the French. Not to be outdone by valor in the face of *mal de mer*, Winnie and Cosmo listed for me the current euphemisms for the verb, *to vomit:* barf, puke, upchuck, ralph, york, and hurl. Vomit, like many of the more polite words in our modern English—fornicate, masturbate, micturate, copulate, and eructate, to name a few— has its roots in the Latin: *vomitare*. And it was not surprising that many of Cosmo and Winnie's favored synonyms were Anglo-Saxon in origin, pithier, consonantal and often uni-syllabic. Then there were the quaintly descriptive phrases they so enjoyed: to pray to the porcelain god, to blow chow, to lose lunch, to blow cookies, to hug the porcelain goddess. Not about to grant them hegemony in the realm of disgusting vocabulary, I described the Roman *vomitaria*, those household chambers prevalent in a civilization of bulimics.

Somewhere in the north Pacific the SS *President Polk* needed to stop at a Japanese harbor, probably Kushiro, to take on water. This was still almost a year before Pearl Harbor, and while things were very tense, this was an American ship, and the Americans were not officially at war.

In the middle of the night, a phalanx of Japanese officers came aboard, demanding that all passengers leave their cabins and come up on deck with their passports. My grandmother and her friend, Violet, and my mother, and Violet's two boys went topside, wrapped in blankets. Bonne Maman did not bring Pierre because he was sound asleep and she knew she couldn't carry him, as he was too heavy. The Japanese officer looked at her passport, which listed two children, and said, "Well—do you have two children or not?"

"Yes," she said.

The officer said, "Then bring him up."

My grandmother said, "No, I cannot do that. He is asleep and I really do not want to wake him. He is a very tiring child, and I had to sing him ever so many lullabies to get him to drop off, and also he is too heavy for me to carry him." Of course she thought *toujours* in French, and spoke excellent but quirky English, but Bonne Maman could only ever sing in French. I always knew exactly what lullaby she must have sung that cold night to my insomniac uncle: *"Fait dodo mon petit Pierre; Fais dodo, tu auras du lolo; Maman est en haut, elle fait du gateaut; Papa est en bas, il fait du chocolat. . . . "*

So the officer, who, according to Bonne Maman, spoke Oxford English, sent a soldier down to her cabin and he carried Pierre on deck, where they all shivered in their dark blue blankets emblazoned with the gold Presidential seal, and the soldiers felt powerful because they were able to disrupt the lives of innocent people and cause them discomfort.

The next morning, notices were slipped under their cabin doors informing the passengers they would be required to deliver a stool sample to Japanese authorities, who, as a service to world health, would be checking for parasites and diseases the passengers might have brought with them from the underdeveloped regions from whence they had come, Cochinchine, Annam, and the Philippines. (Tonkin was not listed because it was already occupied by the sanitary Japanese.) My grandmother and Violet had no intention of reliving— with a jar in hand—those amusing and prolonged moments of potty training their children. So one of the ladies—she never told which one—contributed the specimen that served for both mothers and all four children. Forty years later, Bonne Maman blushed a deep shade of red when she told me this; but her still palpable pleasure in having foiled the Japanese soldiers outweighed her embarrassment.

In all, the trip from Saigon to San Diego took forty-seven

days. A week later, my grandfather Olivier Lévesque and Laurie Gordon also left Saigon and went to Hong Kong. Laurie stayed in China and worked with the Secret Service, and my grandfather went back to the Caltex office in Cairo. Then in December the Japanese bombed Pearl Harbor.

When Mother called from the San Francisco airport, I was reading the letters of Abelard and Heloise, or more specifically I was rereading the letter of Heloise in which she says to Abelard *"God is my witness that if Augustus, Emperor of the whole world, thought fit to honor me with marriage and conferred all the earth on me to possess for ever, it would be dearer and more honorable to me to be called not his Empress but your whore."* That's the 1974 translation; in the 1924 Moncreif translation he has her say *concubine.* I can't help but think the effect is different. Of course it is. It's the same old Latin-versus-Anglo-Saxon paradigm. Concubine, from the Latin *concubinare,* implies a certain, however slight, domesticity; while whore, from the Old English, formerly *hoor* or *hore,* implies a rough and amoral plying of the world's so-called oldest profession. This is what I like about reading different translations of the same thing: confusion and intention. Which is all I will have, since I can no longer read the original Latin.

I had been reading those letters for months, first for mere academic interest in the scholasticism of the early Middle Ages, but then again and again because I was so moved by this extraordinary love Heloise had for Abelard, who, though brilliant, was also arrogant, paranoid, ambitious. After his castration by her uncle and guardian's henchmen,

Abelard distanced himself from Heloise and her requests for closeness of any kind, if only in discussing the details of conventual life. She too was brilliant and learned, and respected by many of the eminent clerics of her time, notably Peter the Venerable. Hers was no puppy worship. This was an intelligent woman loving a man beyond all else, loving him without reserve, loving him unconditionally. How did she do it? I needed to know. What made me think I had to go back over eight hundred years to learn how to give unconditional love, how to let go of anger and resentment? How did Heloise manage not to mind Abelard's paranoid self-absorption? When he claimed that he never saw two clerics together without assuming that they were plotting to persecute him, did she want to shake him, give him a reality check? Apparently not. But such unequivocal love seemed beyond me, even in this less-strenuous twentieth century, where it is unlikely we'll ever be accused of heresy. Once upon a time, I loved my husband the way Heloise loved Abelard: I admired his brilliance and abhorred his critics, I supported his paranoias and would fight his battles with the world; and there were always battles. In her letters, Heloise was not writing of something I did not know; she was writing of something I had lost.

I might have said something to my mother about Abelard and Heloise, because it was a story she knew well, having gone to French schools and having found all the juicy bits to read aloud with her classmates, sitting on the roof in Cairo, or shivering in a Swiss dormitory. She had once taken me to see their tomb in Père Lachaise (their bones are entwined beneath the Gothic scrollery). Although at the time—I was fourteen or so—she skipped some parts of the story, specifically about sex in the convent refectory with the Virgin looking on, and concerning the exact medical details of castration. It was years later, standing in my kitchen overlooking the Hudson, that I said nothing to my mother about Abelard or Heloise, because I realized she was standing in a phone booth in an airport, and all she wanted to talk about was deux cent seize rue Pelerin.

Besides, my parents' marriage is such a model of domestic bliss that I suspect my mother could read Heloise's love letters as a literary or even an erotic exercise, in a way that I could not. My parents are devoted to each other, and always have been; they converse with each other, and genuinely find each other's attempts at wit to be funny. They travel and sometimes go on high-class tours run by Harvard or the Vassar Club or the Museum of Erstwhile Ethnography, across Siberia or into Timbuktu or the Galapagos; and wherever they are, Mother just naturally knows everything about the architecture, the history, and the social mores. And all the widows in the hotel develop crushes on my father and daydream about his enormous white eyebrows. It is a terrible thing to have such well-married parents. I know it is supposed to be very hard on the children when their parents divorce, but as far as I can tell, it is even worse when your parents have a seamless marriage and you grow up thinking this is how your own life will be, and then, alas, discover it is not so.

In the light of all that nuptial bliss, it seems unnecessary to say how beautiful my mother was. When I was very young I knew she was a different fish altogether from the mothers of my classmates at parochial school. Then again, at St. Elmo's Academy she was equally different from the Talbots-clad, Pappagallo-shod maters who could speak with confidence about last week's field hockey debacle. It seemed to me that my mother was more different from them than they were from each other: the pink-and-green-sheathed, lock-jawed women of St. Elmo's, and Saint Agatha's Irish and Italian Catholic mothers with their bobbing BVMs on the dashboard and their uncountable children. At the time I thought it was Mother's foreignness that was off-putting to my peers and their parents—her accent, her taste for inner organs—but later I realized it was her unsettling beauty, which did not immediately appear to be beauty, on account of her broken nose and crooked smile. It only gradually snuck up on you, like French cooking.

All the time I was growing up, I knew the story of my mother's seven suitors; there doesn't seem to be a time when I didn't know, or a time before knowing. It was the integral subtext of the fairy tale about her meeting with my father and their inevitable thereafter—so different from the so-called real life in which nothing I could ever do would ever approach the luminescent pattern of my mother's life.

Why did my mother have seven suitors? Because there are seven continents? That was my assumption, along with Seven Wonders of the World and seven dwarfs. In fact, they only came from three of the seven continents. In Cairo, there was the Muslim prince (or maybe he was a Bey or a

Pasha-in-training, or an Emir or an Aga—that part was always fuzzy) who took my mother picnicking on the pyramids and scuba diving in the Red Sea, and assured her that she would be Wife Number One, and not only that, that she could choose the other three wives.

Ulrich proposed to my mother while they were rowing on Lake Geneva; the young Colette was not quite as expert an oarsman as she was a diver, but she managed to row them ashore when he was overcome by his emotions. She is still quite good friends with Ulrich and his wife, and his sister Yvette. Once my parents took all five of their children to Switzerland and we visited Ulrich and his wife, who is also named Colette. While the adults conversed in a variety of foreign languages, we wandered about the villa looking for dirt, or animals. We found none.

My mother was on her way to college in the states when she met my father. She was a young girl traveling with her parents on the *Queen Elizabeth*, and he was a somewhat older young man traveling with his father on business. The ship wasn't too far out of Southampton when they met, by the very simple device of being seated together at dinner. My father's father also thought that Bonne Maman, the mother of the girl his younger and favored brilliant son was courting, was the most charming and perfect woman he had ever met. Even though Bonne Maman and Grandfather were both married, to other people, and good Catholics, he determined that he would find a way to keep her in his life, forever. That is another story.

At Vassar, my mother initially majored in geology, having

in her treks through the desert learned to love the shape of the earth and its stones and metals and minerals, but the attentions of her professor became so persistent that she had to give up the study of rocks. He wanted to marry her and take her with him on a field trip to Petra in Jordan. She had been to Petra on school trips when she studied with the Jesuits in Cairo. She switched her major to art history.

Mr. Jago initially fell in love with my mother through her portraits. Once, when she was at Vassar, she went home for the summer and discovered that there were exactly sixteen portraits and photographs of herself in her parents' house in Cairo. She claimed she removed them all, which I am sure is true; I am also sure Bonne Maman replaced them as soon as the holidays were over. Mr. Jago was an American who worked for my grandfather at Caltex, and as he was a bachelor they often invited him over, and he fell in love with the dark-haired young woman with the crooked smile in all the portraits. Later, when he was back in New York, he took the train to Poughkeepsie and took Colette out and proposed to her. She said no, which was more or less what he was expecting. A year later when she married my father, Bonne Maman cabled Mr. Jago to let him know, and he sent dozens of white roses on the morning of the wedding, along with a telegram saying he would never marry.

There were three others, of the famous seven suitors, but I don't remember much about them. One was a Texan, and one was English. When my mother mentioned any of them we would imagine ourselves growing up in Texas, wearing oversized hats that weighed five pounds, and eating raw steak, or else living in London and being told every morning that we must speak with a British accent, or else living in Cairo in a huge palace where we were the children of number one wife, and had to play nicely with the children of number two and three wives, and where sometimes baby goats were sacrificed in the courtyard.

After visiting the house on rue Pelerin in Saigon, my parents went on to Cambodia. Sometimes, though rarely, Mother is at a loss for what to say. She told me that she found Cambodia depressing and eerie, and then she realized it was because no one in the country was nearsighted. The Pol Pot had killed everyone who wore glasses.

"I guess our whole family would have been wiped out," I said. "Although they could have saved themselves the trouble and just taken away our glasses. Then we would all have walked off a cliff or into a streetcar sooner or later." Except for Bonne Maman, I thought. She didn't even start wearing reading glasses until she was in her eighties. She may not make sense, but she can see.

"I don't remember seeing any streetcars," my mother pointed out.

"It was just an expression," I said.

"They're calling our flight," my mother said. "Can you hear?" Of course I couldn't hear. She was standing in the middle of an airport and flight announcements over the loudspeaker were but one element of the ambient din.

When we hung up I took off my new glasses and wiped them on the hem of my dress. They are new glasses because they are, at long last, bifocals. In other words, now I can neither see what is far away nor see what is close by. The impressionistic fuzziness of the world has closed in on me, and I don't really mind because what you cannot see clearly loses a bit of its reality, and thus, with the doffing or donning of spectacles, I can control, in this very tiny way, my reality. That is easy for me to say, since I do not live in Cambodia; I can afford this luxury of choice, of hindsight or myopia, strabismus or eagle-vision. With my glasses clean and newly settled upon the bridge of my nose, I can return to Heloise in the twelfth century asking Abelard's advice and instruction upon aspects of conventual life to which, I suspect, she knew the answers perfectly well. Perhaps, like my mother, she was fond of the Socratic method. Perhaps, when the questioner knows what she is doing, it can be a way of expressing love.

What to Wear to See the Pope

Many years ago I stopped minding if they all thought I was spending my life in bed. I stopped flinching when Gus and Cosmo and Winnie remarked that I was allowing the sands of time to run out while I hid between the sheets, surrounded by reading paraphernalia. It no longer bothered me that they found it amusing to suggest I might have narcolepsy, Lyme disease, chronic fatigue syndrome, or a tendency to malinger. As long as I could stay indefinitely under the covers with books of all sizes and shapes and genres and languages, they could say or think anything they pleased. Always always I have liked to read in bed, liked to wear pajamas, liked to dream, and loved to sleep.

So I was in bed, pleased to be wearing plaid flannel, reading Mark Twain's *Personal Recollections of Joan of Arc*, which I found to be profoundly moving. I especially liked Sieur Louis de Conte, the narrator who, from the far vantage point of his old age, speaks of his youth. He describes his contact with greatness and his delight in Joan's pure goodness, as well as her miraculous military intelligence. I always wept when Joan was burned. I was a devotée of Joan of Arc. My bulldog was named for her. Some people actually thought I was lying, or at least making it up when I told them that Mark Twain wrote about Joan of Arc, and that he loved and admired her. "Very funny," said Minnie Bloffadome. "And I suppose Jane Austen really wrote about the Marquis de Sade." Which literary feat, as I get older and more acquainted with the weird and various possibilities of sexual behavior—only through hearsay, of course—does not seem all that impossible.

So I was dozing over Joan of Arc when my husband came in and said "Guess what famous person, that *you* would like to see, is coming to Crykskill?" We lived right next to Crykskill and our house was less than a mile from the border. I could walk there easily, and often did.

"Me as opposed to you? Or me as a member of the human race, or this family?"

"You specifically. You as the only member of this family remotely interested," Gus answered.

"I give up," I said.

"No, really. Guess," he said.

"I don't know," I said. "Who could possibly be coming to Crykskill? I mean, that I would like to see?"

"Think a bit. Who would you like to see?" he said.

"I can't stand it when you make me guess." Then all of a sudden I could think of dozens of people, but they were all dead. Thomas Bernhard, Bernard of Clairvaux, Cocteau, Virginia Woolf, Pierre Abelard, Saint Anthony, Teresa of Avila, What's-his-name—the monk who invented eyeglasses, Greta Garbo. . . . Why couldn't I think of anyone who was alive? "Wittgenstein! Is Wittgenstein dead yet?" I asked Gus.

"He died in 1951, mere months before my birth." Gus knew these things.

"Then I suppose Kafka is also dead. I wouldn't mind meeting Kafka, or at least seeing him from a distance. It might be a little creepy to talk to him, or have dinner with him. Oscar Wilde would be fun. Or the Polar explorers. I would definitely like to meet Scott, or Shackleton."

"You're not trying very hard," Gus said. "It's the Pope. The Pope is coming to Crykskill."

"You're kidding."

"It's in the *Times*."

"I thought he was just going to the City and maybe New Jersey."

"Well, now you know."

Then Gus walked off into that other nighttime inhabited by the awake. I imagined him navigating all the rooms with their lights turned off. He was manic about turning off lights. I liked to have all the rooms lit up like the Fourth of July, or like a wasteful French king's ballroom. I preferred not to bump into things, and not to see what demons were lurking in the corners and what imps were bedeviling under the sofa. Although I had pointed out that we were talking about a few cents' worth of electricity—or even dollars, so what?—this remained something that we fought about, irrationally and breathlessly. I knew more or less what Gus did in his night-time. He sat in the darkness and watched old movies; he was especially fond of Japanese war films and contemporary pornography. Or he went and sat in a chair at the end of the field, and looked at the stars and the stealth bombers streaking up the Hudson on their way to West Point, and he drank a twenty-year-old Armagnac that was possibly the most delicious thing we would ever taste in our lives. Knowing all that, I also knew there was a mystery to his nighttime awakeness, something that kept us quite separate.

I imagined what it would be like when I went to see the Pope in Crykskill. First I had to imagine what I would wear. My initial instinct was to go all in black, like an Old World widow, but I decided against that, because black was what I wore most of the time anyway and therefore would not have been special enough. If my goal was to be elegant yet monastic, chic yet spiritual, which it most certainly was, and if I had rejected black as the predominant color scheme, then it seemed to me I was left with brown. Very dark brown. And nothing with a cowl: that would have been too obviously derivative. I had a terrific Italian brown suit with a velvet collar: a definite possibility. Then I realized that if I wanted to wear Bonne Maman's antique Coptic cross, which I did, I would have to wear something without buttons in front, a turtleneck or a jewel-neck blouse. Normally I wore a yellow silk blouse with the brown suit, for a somewhat autumnal look. But this Coptic cross was inset with an amethyst, which would clearly not go with any yellow. The cross was both a fond reminder of my grandparents' and mother's years living in Egypt and redolent of Mother's battles with the Catholic diocese over the size and shape of the tombstone of my grandfather, Bon Papa. Of course I knew that shades of purple, especially the darker ones, such as mauve, magenta, violet, plum, and puce were regarded as episcopal, and frequently worn, either for the chasuble or as an accent, on Lenten occasions. But the Color Consultant at Saks, to whom my mother had taken me—unwilling and cynical—had said that purple was definitely not in my personal spectrum. It was, however, in my mother's. But I liked to think I was not a slave to the dicta of fashion. Hadn't I always worn yellow, even though from an early age it had been drilled into me that blondes must never do that?

Color was one thing. But it was also important that clothes have a name, a very specific name. A sheath and a gored skirt were two of my favorites, for reasons that had nothing to do with their lines, everything to do with their names. There were also peplums, pelerines, boleros, and Capri pants. There were cloches, toques, and turbans. If I could wear just one article of clothing that had a specific, as opposed to a generic, name, I knew I would feel better prepared. Of course I could not wear a wimple. It would not be appropriate and it would too clearly reveal my childhood fantasies. Still, I liked to think I was an aficionado of wimples in their infinite variety. I realized this was not going to be simple.

I imagined that I would ride my bike along the aqueduct path to wherever the Pope was officiating. This part of the plan pleased me enormously, because we already knew that one of the big problems with the Pope's visit would be the parking and traffic jams in the city. There was a Gridlock Alert for all of Manhattan for all four days. I loved the sound of that: Gridlock Alert. It was so specific and weird; a mere one hundred years ago it didn't exist, neither the concept nor the phrase. And in another hundred years, how would it be seen, as a quaint literary anachronism, like a barouche or a periwig? Or would it still be impossible to move in any direction at Fifth and Forty-Seventh at noontime? So I would ride my bike and not have to worry about gridlock or parking. My choice of attire would be affected by the decision to ride a bike, I thought. Not that a short skirt was suitable for seeing the Pope, but the fact of bicycling decisively kiboshed that choice.

Perhaps I would even bring Saint Joan, and she too would be blessed by the Pope. In that case I would have to walk, because she was remarkably lazy and slow, even for a bulldog. She could never have kept up with my bike, no matter how slowly I pedaled. Bulldogs have short legs, sausage-like torsos, massive heads, prodigious jowls, and respiratory trouble; like all dogs they can only sweat through their tongues, but this breed produces excessive puddles of saliva. It was possible that she would even have trouble walking two or three miles south on the aqueduct. This was something to consider.

Each year for the feast of St. Francis of Assisi, anyone in our village, of any denomination, could bring his pet down to St. Bruno's Catholic Church to be blessed. On those occasions, rather than walking the less than a mile to town, I would drive Saint Joan because I didn't want both of us to be embarrassed when she collapsed in a puddle of her own drool on the church steps. That way we could arrive without undue perspiration.

Last year I sat on the stone wall and chatted with some altar boys, while Saint Joan lay flat out, all four legs splayed, in all four directions, north, east, south, and west, as only bulldogs can do to such effect. There were all sorts of dogs waiting to be blessed, including the kind that have blue-black tongues. One particular dog was quite willing to show off his tongue. I realized that it was the exact same shade of dark blue as the blue lipstick my daughter Winnie sometimes wore on school mornings. It was not a lip color I could appreciate, but perhaps she saw it as an antidote to my insufferable morning cheerfulness. It was hard to see my daughter with blue lips in the morning and not call her Ophelia, and I did not resist the urge.

As I sat there on the stone wall, loosely tethered to Saint Joan who did not have to feign her indifference to the surrounding children, a rather gaunt man placed his cat-suitcase next to me. I noticed that most of the cats-to-be-blessed were secured inside these traveling cages, which was fine by me, since Saint Joan found cats a bit unnerving on account of their claws and their quickness. Several little girls came by and looked through the grill of the cat-suitcase.

One of the girls said to her father, "Dad, you better look at this cat."

The father glanced over and said quickly, "Yes, a nice cat."

The daughter said, more insistently, "No, I mean you better LOOK at that cat."

The father said, "Honey, I'm trying to talk."

The girl said, "But the cat has only one eye."

This caught her father's attention, and he looked through the grill, and nodded and said, "Just one eye."

"Where's the other one?" she asked him, but her father took her hand and was pulling her toward the other side of the church steps.

Meanwhile, more children were looking through the grill into the shadows of the cat-suitcase, to see the one-eyed cat. I knew I would have to look myself, sooner or later, but I have always been a little squeamish about blood and guts, and I imagined a gaping socket and perhaps some exposed nerves, or perhaps a less definable wound simply oozing pus. The gaunt man who had deposited the cat next to me on the wall was nowhere to be seen. I assumed he was hoping for a miraculous cure. But when I did look, there was no wound of any kind. The cat simply had one eye; where the other eye would have been in any other cat was smooth gray fur, just like the rest of him. I couldn't imagine that his owner would want to ruin that uni-ocular perfection with a prosthetic eye; so I suppose he was there just for the general benefits of blessing, like the rest of us.

There was also a sweet six-month-old Basset hound with a face already ancient with wisdom; he was named, regrettably, Elvis.

I had never given much thought to my outfit for the Saint Francis Day blessing, recognizing that the animals were the important ones and they were already attired.

But this would be different. This mattered in ways I was unwilling to articulate. If I saw the Pope, and did it properly, then perhaps I would emerge not only blessed but somehow wiser, somehow able to finally tell the difference between what mattered and what did not. So I continued wondering what to wear when I went to see the Pope. Hadn't Brigitte Bardot worn a mantilla when she'd had an audience the week before? (Not that I classed myself with Brigitte Bardot, for a host of reasons.) I wished I knew what had happened to all the mantillas we used to wear on Sunday mornings. My mother never threw anything away, so perhaps they were in the barn somewhere, wrapped in tissue paper, in an old leather suitcase, neatly labeled.

I tried visualizing the scene, and so whenever I imagined going to see the Pope I pictured myself with sunglasses, prescription of course. This was because of the eye problems that had plagued our household for months. In fact, the Pope was not coming a moment too soon.

First there was Clarissa, an endearing and comical sixteen-year-old from Strasbourg who had lived us with all summer in one of those trans-Atlantic child exchanges. Clarissa's left-eye problem had started out as red and puffy, then it became swollen and even pooled over with liquid of some kind. It began up at Lake Winnitonka where we all swam for hours each day because it was deadly hot, and so at first we thought it was just swimmer's eye. But it kept on being red, and got redder. The veins in her eyeball became prominent and enlarged, and then the eyeball itself started to swell so that we thought it would pop itself right out of the socket. All this time we were visiting and sailing and going to the beach, and we kept thinking it would go away the next day. It never did. When I finally took Clarissa to my elderly ophthalmologist, I could tell he was appalled that this eye condition had gone untreated for so long. I was mortified. Then I sent Clarissa on the plane back to Strasbourg with that terribly red and swollen eye, and, what was worse, I could not even enter the terminal at JFK because of a Level 5 Terrorist Alert, which is the highest level. I could not believe I was sending this beautiful child with an oozing swollen eyeball into an alien and crowded airport teeming with both security agents and terrorists, who all looked more or less the same and equally dangerous.

Clarissa's eye was better now. Her mother wrote that she had seen a Parisian specialist who said Clarissa must of course have contracted this nasty virus at Lake Winnitonka, since in all of Europe it was *complètement* unknown and *unheard of*. This doctor reminded me of Jonathan Swift, who also liked to grant a New World provenance to all things appalling.

Not long afterwards my son Cosmo had come back from soccer camp with conjunctivitis, or so I diagnosed his chronic red inflamed eye. Feeling extremely penitent on account of my slowness vis-à-vis Clarissa's eye, I wanted to rush Cosmo to the doctor right away. But Cosmo had always been extremely resistant to visiting doctors, and so for two weeks, while the veins of his right eyeball became more and more pronounced, he managed to be entirely busy during every hour that coincided with the doctor's office hours. Finally one evening I could no longer bear it, and in the middle of cooking dinner I took him off to the Oates Landing Hospital Emergency Room, where we spent several hours in the waiting room watching *Jeopardy* (the category was Popes: *He called for the Second Vatican Council in 1962. Who is Pope John XXIII? Too easy. He reformed the Julian calendar and established leap years. Who is Gregory XIII?*) and watching the one and only doctor fill out forms and lick her pencil's eraser. By ten o'clock we had some broad-spectrum antibiotic drops and went home hungry.

Perhaps my sense of urgency was exacerbated by the poison ivy on my own eyes and eyelids. I itched constantly, and had fantasies of scooping out my entire itchy eyeball with a spoon. It became clear that I had no patience or tolerance for itchy eyes. I was cranky and morbid. I walked around with cotton soaked in witch hazel held to my eyes, sometimes both at once. It was not hard to imagine the darkness creeping upon me.

Hundreds of years ago my brother James and I spent hours in the lovely broken-down barn, playing the Either/Or game. It was exploratory rather than competitive. (In retrospect, it briefly occurred to me that our choices would define our later selves, but then it seemed better not to explore that.) In the Either/Or game, you merely chose between two unpleasant alternatives. Would you rather be deaf or blind? Would you rather lose a leg or an arm? Would you rather die in a fire or on an iceberg? Would you rather drown or fall out of an airplane? With whom would you rather be alone on a desert island: Uncle Harold or Aunt Winifred? Would you rather go completely bald or grow a beard? (The horrificness of these two options was only significant for girls. I was still ignorant of the vast lore of bearded female saints.) Would you rather have a hunchback or a clubfoot? Would you rather get leprosy and live forty years watching your fingers fall off, or die painfully of the bubonic plague, with pus oozing from every sore? Would you rather vomit or have diarrhea? Having begun the game with fairly obvious choices, we searched for more and more disgusting and unpleasant alternatives.

Our knowledge of diseases and afflictions came mostly from the nuns at Saint Agatha's school. But I was also personally well acquainted with the more arcane forms of torture and death, having piously studied the lives of the saints. I suspected that this obscure but titillating cache of information was often the reason why James chose to play Either/Or with me, even when he had other options. It kept me going back to my *Lives of the Saints*, for more, and more. Would you rather be crucified upside-down like Peter, or stoned to death like Stephen and Timothy? Would you rather have your bowels removed by being slowly wound upon a windlass, as in the Catherine wheel, or your breasts chopped off, as Agatha's were? (No one playing the game had breasts or anything approximating breasts, but this torture was delightfully illustrated in one of my books.) Would you rather be beheaded (as were so many young Christian women), or drowned with a millstone tied around your neck? Would you rather be tied in a net and tossed to a raging bull, like Blandina, or thrown directly to the wild beasts in an arena, like Felicity, Perpetua, and so many others?

While we enjoyed all the grim possibilities of martyrdom, what grounded the game for us and what we kept coming back to was the most basic choice: whether to be deaf or blind? James was tone-deaf and colorblind. We had been told he could never be a fighter pilot. I was extremely astigmatic and had already been in for my first eye surgery, during which the doctors took the eyeball out of its socket, tightened up the muscles behind it, and then popped the eyeball back in. James and I always said we'd rather be deaf.

Then there was Saint Joan. She always had eye problems, notably *Entropion* and *secondary veterinary districiasis,* which meant her eyelids folded in so that external skin and cilia touched and irritated her eyeball. This was a not-uncommon genetic disorder in bulldogs, on account of their wrinkles of extra skin, although I was sure she did not see any of it as extra. Saint Joan also had conjunctivitis most of the time, so her right eye oozed fairly constantly, and occasionally she developed cysts just under her eyelids. As for the pus, I wiped it away every morning with a Q-tips. It was a bit like the ritual wiping of the crusty sleep from your infant's eyes; which is to say, I enjoyed it. But when the cysts developed, more radical measures were called for and we had to apply creams and ointments. And though she *was* saintly, Saint Joan sometimes balked, and snarled at the sight of a pharmacological tube.

Not that I thought the Pope would have anything to do or say about any of this, but it did seem amazing to me just how rampant had been infections of the eye among us.

Then I had a dream, and in my dream the Pope was a boy, or rather there was a child Pope, and he came to visit me. He was a child Pope the way a boy can be the new Dalai Lama, the chosen one. There is, in fact, no tradition in the Catholic church of there being a child Pope, although there is the story of Pope Joan, the young woman around 800 or 900 A.D. who, for reasons of feminine safety, had spent her life pretending to be a man and living in a monastery. She became so well-known and sought-after for her wisdom that she was unanimously elected to the Papacy. She died, rather painfully, in childbirth, just two years later. Most historians say the story is apocryphal, but I prefer to believe it. Although there was a time many, many years ago, when I confused this Pope Joan with Joan of Arc, which is understandable only in the light of my egregious ignorance, as there really is no connection between them except that they both dressed as men. Which in fact is an enormous connection. It had a lot to do with why the English bishops were so determined to burn Joan: her unwillingness to give up men's clothing.

In the dream, my friend Kevin, who is religious but not Catholic, had been to school with this child Pope and, intuitively knowing that I would like to meet him, Kevin brought the child Pope over to my house one day during his New York visit. The Pope was pale and slightly pudgy, in the way that young boys often are before they have their big pubertal growth spurt. His voice cracked; it sounded as if he had an incipient sore throat, or allergies. (Of course his voice was cracking because of that very puberty. But I didn't realize it in the dream, any more than I had realized it when it happened to Cosmo.) We visited for a while, and the Pope seemed like a nice young man. Then it was dinnertime and I made pasta with pesto for the children, and although Kevin and the Pope kept saying that they couldn't stay for dinner, it turned out they really were hungry and so I gave them pasta with pesto and tomato salad. Then it was time for the Pope to go, and we went outside. It turned out that we lived right on the river. A speedboat was approaching, and in it were two men dressed completely in dark clothes, and carrying machine guns. I thought, *That is not very much security for the Pope,* but I didn't say anything. We all went down to our dock. Just before the Pope was about to climb aboard the boat, I asked Kevin if the boy Pope would mind if I kissed his ring, and Kevin said, *I think he would like you to.* So I knelt on the dock and kissed his ring.

In the morning I remembered this dream remarkably well. In my fondness for slumber, I often tend to sleep through my dreams as well as through the memory of dreams. But this one I remembered and wrote down. But it was only when I got to the very end of it that I saw what I'd been wearing while the boy Pope was in my house. Pajamas. I was not dressed exactly like a man or a boy, just in pajamas, which anyone can wear. Only in the dream they were not pajamas, they were thin silk trousers and a long tunic, like the *Ao dai* worn in Indochina. And they were dark purple, Concord grape purple. There was something around my neck, but I could not picture if it was a cross. It may have been an amber pendant with a prehistoric fly captured inside. I don't know why I thought that, except that perhaps in my dream the boy Pope had said something about insects and the value of all living things. Something that Francis of Assisi might have said.

After that, it was much easier to imagine the Pope, to imagine my journey and his blessing, because at last I knew what I would be wearing. I rarely felt better about anything upon recalling a dream. Usually I would be disturbed to be faced yet again with the weird dross and kinkiness of my subconscious. But this dream was my personal set of instructions, my benediction and my absolution: I would wear purple, for liturgical rather than fashion reasons. And I would wear the long pants and tunic of an *Ao dai*, which would be somewhat androgynous as well as a subtle homage to the brave Martyrs of Indochina (those Beatified Dominicans who suffered horribly in the early nineteenth century, and whose feast day it would soon be). At any rate, with pants I would be able to circumspectly ride my bicycle.

But when the day finally came, Saint Joan and I walked along the aqueduct, slowly, slowly. We arrived only minutes before the Pope was delivered by helicopter to his waiting Pope-mobile. Some might have said I was overdressed for the occasion, but for once I did not doubt myself, or my attire.

Souvenir Staples

This time around, I wanted something to show for all the trouble and expense.

I had been passive for a long time, if not like a rug, then like the tense. My other tense was conditional. I always asked politely, as I had been taught was the only way one could ask, *if I could please if it's not too much trouble see the cystic teratoma that had just been removed from my ovary. I would like to see it, if I may, if I might.*

That got me nowhere. This time I didn't want to merely see it. I wanted to get it back. It was my teratoma, and I wanted to keep it forever in a jar on my mantel.

This teratoma, from the Greek *teratos,* for monster, and *oma,* for tumor, was a growth, perhaps a monstrous growth, containing embryonic elements of germ layers. But it was mine. It was presumably attached to one or both ovaries. And if it was anything like the earlier teratomas, it would be filled with blond hair, and of course blood and pus.

What amazed me then and amazes me still is that more than once before I'd had this same operation and had proprietary teratomas removed, yet at no time did I suggest, never mind insist on keeping the monstrous hairy growth that had caused all the trouble.

It's not that I was suddenly less polite. I was desperate. I wanted something tangible. I wanted more proof than yet another incision and a doctor's bill. What did I know? What if I was still inhabited by mutant blonde embryos? What if there never was anything at all?

To this end, I asked my doctor if I could, please, have the teratoma to keep when they were finished with it. I was very fond of my doctor. He had silver hair, wore perfect blue suits, and spoke with one of those Central European accents that seemed to have no specific provenance. He told me it was not normal procedure to return removed organs or tumors. I said I suspected as much, but I wanted it anyway. He gave me the phone number of the hospital's pathology lab, as the teratoma would be in their purview.

I called Pathology, and explained that I was going in for surgery and wanted to have my teratoma back after they were finished with it. The man with whom I spoke said it was impossible.

I said, "How can it be impossible?"

"Because we don't release human tissue," he said.

"But that's not the same as impossible," I said. "That's just a technicality."

"We don't do it," he said.

"Is there a supervisor I could speak with, please?" I asked.

He put me on hold for a very long time, and finally the supervisor, a woman named Lillian, came on. I explained, again, that I just wanted to keep my teratoma when they were through with it.

"We don't release human tissue," she said. "It's against the law."

"But it's mine," I said. "It's in my body now, and that's not illegal."

"It's against the law to release human tissue," she repeated.

"I don't get it," I said. "If I were having my leg amputated, couldn't I take that home?"

"We never release human tissue," she said.

"Well, what do you release?" I asked.

"We often give back breast implants, because people want them for litigation. And sometimes when people have hip or joint replacements we give them back the old screws. Also the stuff that kids swallow, pennies and toys and stuff," she said.

"I would really like to have this teratoma," I said. "It only seems fair, since I have to go through the trouble of having it removed."

"I wish I could help you," she said. "But I can't."

"I don't think you understand," I said. "This teratoma is mine now, like my hair or my toenails or my kneecap. I don't plan on giving it away, so it will still be mine. Therefore, it's not as if you're giving me something that wasn't mine before."

"I just know it's against the law to release human tissue."

"What about private property?" I said. "What about my inalienable rights?"

"I realize you're upset about this," Lillian said to me.

"Upset?" I repeated. "I suppose I am. For goodness sakes,"

I said. "I've never even seen it. Does it seem fair to you that all sorts of people will see it, and I won't?"

"Well, I think we could take a Kodachrome for you," she said.

Later, I wondered if it would have helped if I'd told Lillian that I had already chosen the clear glass jar where I planned to keep the teratoma. It was a lovely jar of old New England glass, with a woman's head and neck for a stopper. Or should I have mentioned how perfect it would look on the marble mantel between the girondelles in the shape of Persian maidens? Would it have helped my cause had I made it clear just how much this was not an idle request? Not for the first time, I was experiencing *l'esprit de l'escalier,* and fruitlessly. But then, it was always fruitless.

And that was how we left it, with Lillian saying she would do her best to remember to take a picture of this particular hairy lump that would be delivered one afternoon to Pathology with my name on it. When I hung up, I was sweating. It seemed to me that I had been very demanding, even borderline rude, and I was filled with a nervous fear that I would be reprimanded. And just to prove the point, that *there is never a good reason to be rude,* as my mother often said, and my mother is almost always right about almost everything, look at what I accomplished: nothing. Since I knew perfectly well that the Kodachrome was a sop that I would never see.

On the operating table, like the proverbial slab of meat, I tried one last time, as politely as I could, given my disadvantaged position. Also, I was hoping to be covered soon with a preheated blanket and wearing a pair of oversized socks.

There were two medical students, Sam and Leah. I assumed they were there to watch, and although I didn't begrudge them the educational experience, I was dismayed to think that here were two more strangers who would be privy to my inner organs. They were so anxious and solicitous that it seemed the only thing to do was be solicitous in return. What on earth made me think I had to engage in polite conversation? Couldn't I have just lain there and wept?

Sam was trying to put the IV line in the anterior ulnar vein of my left hand, and even without my glasses I could see that his hands were shaking. Really shaking. I didn't want to be stabbed unnecessarily, or have the IV improperly inserted. I thought of saying something helpful, but he was so nervous that I feared to make him worse.

"You have such delicate veins," he said. I nodded, although I knew perfectly well that that was completely false. I have fairly obvious and easily punctured veins. Nurses have complimented me on my veins, how readily they yield up the vial of blood or accept the IV.

He seemed to need some soothing, so I asked him what his favorite rotation had been, thus far in medical school.

He said, "I thought I wanted to be a pathologist. But now I'm thinking about surgery."

"I was just chatting with your pathology department," I told him. Surgery seemed a bad idea.

"You were?"

"I wanted to get this teratoma back, when you guys are finished with it. Perhaps you know someone powerful in Pathology."

"I don't know anyone powerful," he said. He was still struggling with the IV.

"I just read a great book by a pathologist," I told him. "I think you would like it. It's a collection of essays about various aspects of the preservation of bodily parts. He writes about mummies, and medieval medicine, and anatomical museums in Italy, and relics, and autopsies. I guess that is a lot of what pathologists do, autopsies."

"Actually," Sam said. "Did you know that an autopsy is the only thing you get for free in the hospital?"

"Really?" I said. "I wasn't planning on having one."

"No, of course not," he said quickly, a little nervously. "But isn't it amazing? You have to pay for every little thing here, but not an autopsy. And they cost thousands of dollars, once you slice up everything and test it."

"But you don't autopsy everyone who dies?" I asked. "Or do you?"

"Oh, no. Not nearly so many as we'd like," said Sam. "It's because they're so expensive. But they're always interesting, when we do get to do them."

"I'm glad to hear that," I said.

The IV tube was still not in my vein, and I was happy to see that Sam's efforts had become half-hearted and that he was resigned to letting someone else perform this task.

Leah had just finished an ophthalmology internship, and she told us that her favorite medical procedure was eye surgery. Especially cataract removal. She said it was quite spectacular to watch, because it was so delicate and it happened so quickly, and the patient never even went to sleep. I thought that the bloody removal of this teratoma was a far cry from a quick, delicate cataractectomy, and to compensate, I told Leah about my own eye surgery, albeit more than thirty years ago. Back then, in order to remedy my strabismus, the eyeballs were removed from their sockets so that the muscles connecting them to my brain could be tightened up. Or something like that. Then the eyeballs were popped back into their sockets. That was what my doctor had told me, and that was what I'd always believed. When it was over, my eyes no longer wandered randomly about the room. I assumed that Leah would inform me that this type of surgery was no longer performed in such a primitive fashion, but I was wrong. She said that's still how they do it. They lever out the eyeball and rewind the muscle, as if it was a slack yo-yo string, and then reinsert in the socket. Voilà.

I'm not sure how we got onto the subject of glass eyes, although it's not hard to imagine the sequence. Not hard, because I took every opportunity offered to tell this story about Frederick Woolsey. He had two glass eyes and only one empty socket. The pupil on one of the eyes was dilated, and on the other was the normal diameter. Depending upon whether he was in a darkened room or not, or whether he was hanging around with a lot of stoned people, he would pop in the appropriate eyeball. He kept the other one in a velvet-lined case in his vest pocket. Frederick was a very unusual boy. He went to St. Elmo's Boys School back when I was at St. Elmo's Girls School across the street, so it could not be said that I actually knew him. Though of course we all knew all about him. He wore a black wool cape all year round, carried a silver-headed cane, and revered the Romantic poets. A few years after graduation he died in a small plane just as it flew over Missolonghi, which just so happened to be where Byron died while fighting with the Greek independence movement. Most of Frederick's class-mates assumed it was suicide.

Leah told me that glass was no longer used for glass eyes or rather for ocular prostheses. Now they're made of some kind of plastic.

It had been a long wait stretched out on that metal table, and I was not sorry when my handsome doctor told me, in his endearing and seductive accent, that he preferred Mozart for surgery like this.

It seemed rather harsh, and a bit illogical, that every single nurse, medical student, intern, anesthesiologist, and surgeon in that theater would see more of my internal organs than I ever would. And I was the one who was expected to live with them, or what would be left of them, forever, or for a certain amount of time, for better or worse, in sickness and health, till death did us part. Then the anes-thesiologist did something to the IV and told me to count backwards from ten, and at nine and a half Sam asked me how to spell the name of the author of the pathology essays, and I think I managed to spell it all out, a hyphenated multi-syllabic name, but I will never be sure.

It was the same day when I woke up. I was alone in a gray, unlit room and it was impossible to move my body a cen-timeter in any direction without incurring waves of pain, like heavy machinery. I was not happy to discover that there was a tube emerging from my right nostril. I thought I had specifically asked that I not wake up with an NG tube, and here it was, stuck all the way down the back of my throat and into my stomach, and spewing out bile into a clear bucket next to my bed. This was dismaying, but I was heavily drugged, which is the best way to be when your middle has been sliced open, your vital organs messed with, and there is only a nasal gastric tube to keep you entertained.

After a while I realized that I was not alone. My husband, Gus, was in the room with me. He was talking on the phone to the children. There was a crisis. A terrible thunderstorm was roaring that night. Rain was sluicing down city streets, while upriver in our little village the thunder was ruining sleepy dreams and lightning was gashing the night sky. And Saint Joan, our beloved bulldog, was terrified of thunderstorms. Whenever thunder roared overhead, she shook uncontrollably and then crashed into our bedroom. Her heart pounded so that I believed I could hear it above the screeching arias that we put on the stereo to drown out the thunderclaps. Sometimes I helped her up onto our bed, something she could never manage alone, chunky thing that she was. Even when we tucked her under the eiderdown, she shook so much that we held onto the mattress for dear life, so it seemed.

I knew that we had tranquilizers for her, if only someone could find them and give them to her in time. I tried to tell Gus to tell Winnie where the tranquilizers were, on the second to lowest shelf on the bookcase between the pantry and the kitchen, in a basket next to the thirteen volumes of the OED, and just below all the gardening and bug books, in a bottle marked specifically *For Saint Joan in a thunderstorm.* It was a Controlled Substance called Meprobamate, and a bright orange label warned that it could cause dizziness or drowsiness. But no matter. Apparently I never articulated those directions, and it was not clear if I said anything at all, or just dreamed that from my hospital bed I could still come up with solace and comfort for my dog and children when the elements were threatening.

The next day the dressing was removed from my abdomen, and if I put my glasses on I could see the incision. I started counting the staples. I counted very carefully and came up with seventeen. It was remarkably challenging thing to count a simple row of staples. First of all, I was more or less horizontal and the staples were on more or less the same plane. Second of all, since the incision was not geometrically straight and in fact curved a bit like the Saw Mill Parkway, staples could get lost behind turnings. Last and most difficult was the problem of the belly button, formerly an innie, now unidentifiable, where several staples were bunched together and not visible from my vantage point. But having little else to do, I counted the staples several times, making digital contact with each one, and when I came up with seventeen three times in a row, I felt confident that I had accounted for all of them.

My sister Sophie came to visit, and, being an experienced hospital visitor, she immediately took my chart from its slot at the foot of the bed and began to read. She found something there she had not seen before, which was the Pain Scale, the Sedation Scale, and the Wong/Baker Faces Rating Scale. The concept behind these ratings intrigued and entertained us for quite a while. The Pain Scale went from zero to five, zero being *No Pain* and five being *Worst Possible Pain.* In between were *Mild Pain, Moderate Pain, Severe Pain,* and *Very Severe Pain.* What was *The Worst Possible Pain,* we wondered? Who would ever be sure enough to describe their pain as the *Worst Possible?* Wasn't that unknowable? And being superstitious, I was pretty sure that I for one would never risk describing my discomfort as the *Worst Possible,* any more than I would ever take off in a plane without crossing myself.

The Sedation Scale went from one to five, and then to SL, for *Sleep.* One was *Wide Awake,* then there was *Drowsy,* then *Dozing Intermittently,* then *Mostly Sleeping* and five was *Awakens Only When Aroused.*

"If SL indicates a sleeping patient," Sophie said, "What does D stand for?"

"Dead," I answered, because we think alike in these things.

"I would not take it amiss to be classified as *Awakens Only When Aroused,*" said Sophie.

And then there was the Wong/Baker Faces Rating Scale, for which, apparently, words were inadequate, and therefore these were indicated by line drawings. Sophie demonstrated for me. Zero was a perfectly hemispheric smile and arched eyebrows; by number three the mouth line was drooping at the edges and the eyebrows were getting pointy; number five was desolate, with a perfectly hemispheric frown, and deeply indented eyebrows pressing upon weeping eyes.

"You're in deep trouble when you look like number five," said Sophie, and she was right.

I think that was the day I counted my staples for the millionth time, and came up with twenty. I counted several times, slowly and methodically, and each time there were twenty. I was somewhat more mobile by then, and could sit up enough to get a more aerial view of the path of the incision. I imagined myself setting off the metal detector at airport security. I imagined baring my belly and hearing the resounding oohs and aahs of the security guards.

But no. What was initially a rather appealing scenario quickly became realistic, and humiliating, and yet more evidence of my inability to negotiate even the simplest instance of an x-ray machine.

Because of such compelling activities, it was at least two or three days after the Mad Cows hit the news media that I realized I was at risk for Bovine Spongiform Encephalopathy. Because of the morphine, which I was loath to give up, it took me a while to calculate the number of years since I had last eaten British beef and if it was recent enough for me to be at risk for possible onset of the madness. It was. Worse than that, Winnie was at risk as well.

We had gone to stay with Tippit in London in 1990 when Winnie was ten. Tippit, who made beautiful films and very few meals, wanted to celebrate our arrival with a chunk of British beef. I remembered it all so well. We had to remove a dead mouse from her oven and I was so grateful we had found the little carcass before baking it. I knew about incinerated mice, the smells they give off, from personal experience. Winnie sweetly volunteered to take the mouse, hastily encased in a Mueslix box, and bury it in the back garden. We acquiesced and never wondered what she would use for a shovel. Then I showed Tippit how to cook roast beef, and we all ate with appetite.

I did not want to die of a perforated brain. I did not want to die at all. All I wanted was to go home with my own teratoma that was full of blond hair that I had grown on my own ovary. I wanted this tangible and visible explanatory evidence of the weirdness of human anatomy. The more the nurses and Pathology told me this was not possible, the more anxious I became.

Plus, I objected to their misuse of the language. Of course it was *possible*; it was not *allowed*. Hadn't I spent years correcting my children as to the uses of Can and May? Can I go to Terry's house? Yes, you are physically capable of going to Terry's house. Would you like to know if you have permission to go there? The impulse to explain this distinction to the hospital staff was becoming overwhelming. I knew I should be stopped.

When my brother Olivier came to visit, I was sitting up in bed and intaking clear liquids. When you were put on a clear liquid diet in the hospital, this meant you got reconstituted chicken broth and Jell-O for breakfast, lunch, and dinner. It was not a menu designed to whet the appetite; it was barely an improvement over the potassium and saline solution flowing directly into your veins. Olivier was starving, as he often was when a meal had receded more than two hours into the distant past, and I had no food to offer him. But he did find the box full of latex surgical gloves and proceeded to blow up several and tie them off at the wrist. Soon there was a pile of inflated fingers on the floor. It was hard not to perceive it as a midden of the amputated hands of thieves with edema. When the telephone rang Olivier picked it up and I immediately knew we were about to plummet down the long chute of regression into stupid jokes we found funny as children. This was a hazard of spending time with siblings, and one of the best reasons for ensuring that familial visits be spent in private; it was also an excellent way to infuriate, alienate, and even disgust one's in-laws. Which was not always a bad idea. So Olivier answered the phone with a curt "Intensive Care." Then I watched the pleasure on his face as it became clear that he had caused a kind and solicitous friend to go into a panic. The next time the phone rang, he barked out "Yellow Fever Ward." Again, he was convulsed with pleasure. I loved watching him. And if it hurt the incision to laugh, all I had to do was press the button on my Patient Controlled Analgesia pump. Then things got out of hand.

"What's the worst thing I could say?" Olivier asked me.

"Proctology," I suggested.

"Or Pathology," he said.

"Don't remind me," I said.

"What about Urology?" Olivier said.

"Epistemology!"

"Teleology!"

"Ontology!"

We thought we were hilarious. "How long do you think you'll be here?" Olivier asked me.

"I don't know," I said.

"Promise that you'll always answer the phone with one of them," he said.

Of course I lied, and promised.

Then one day the IV was pulled out and I could no longer dose myself with morphine, and it was time to go home, empty-handed. And suddenly nothing happened as it was supposed to; instead of getting better, the pain became worse and worse; I began to reconsider the classification of Worst Possible. Percocet every six hours was not doing the trick; certainly it could not match the heft of morphine every six minutes. It was time to bargain with God.

These were negotiations to be taken seriously. I didn't want to promise something I wouldn't keep, such as going to mass absolutely every Sunday or making a pilgrimage to Lourdes. So I worked out a deal that included many good works and a small shrine in the woods outside my house, which I could build myself with all the rocks I dug up when I was putting in the vegetable garden. Then I closed my eyes and prayed, until I realized that I could no longer remember the whole of the Lord's Prayer in French; I would get as far as *Sancifié soit son nom,* and then I couldn't get any further. I knew how important it was that I say it correctly.

This seemed to go on for days. Sometimes I dozed off and half-dreamed that pain relief was simply a matter of getting the words right and spelling the pain correctly, or saying it in another language, and then it would go away. When I woke up, this would stay with me for a while. I would keep thinking: *Of course, that's all it is, just articulating the right word in the right language. With the right word the pain will naturally go away.*

Meanwhile my mother came to stay. She rearranged the furniture in the living room, and answered the phone, and kept her Ferragamos away from Saint Joan who would never chew anything unless she was provoked. But if she ever did chew anything, it always seemed to be my mother's expensive Italian shoes.

I lay in bed and hoped the pain would abate. When there were good moments, I would count my staples again. I had finally settled on twenty-two. What reassured me was that Winnie also counted twenty-two, and there was nothing wrong with her.

My mother couldn't stand to look at my incision except through the macro lens of her camera. The film in her camera, she said, was especially good for skin tones. Twenty years ago she had taken pictures of Olivier's hernia scar; now she was going to photograph mine. She had me lie on the carpet in my bedroom; it was morning and the sun was streaking in through the south windows and onto my pasty, distended abdomen. She took several pictures of the incision, and never winced so long as she had the camera in front of her face.

One day I went in town to see my charming doctor and ensure that the incision was healing properly. He said it was. None of the twenty-two staples was infected.

For days my mother cooked comfort food for my children, and rearranged more furniture. Sometimes she sat in the red armchair in my bedroom and lamented various slippages of modern life. It especially bothered her that no one wore black to funerals anymore. My mother always wore all-black to funerals, either a suit or a dress, and by all-black she meant stockings, shoes, and undergarments. It was one of my mother's finer points that she firmly believed that God could see, and cared to see, that which was hidden from human eyes.

Just two weeks previously she had attended the funeral of Herbert, the husband of her old friend Gladys, and she was quite disturbed that Gladys had worn a skirt and sweater to the funeral mass.

"What color were they?" I asked.

"Not black," she said. "Perhaps that's what happens when you live in Maine for too many years."

I nodded from my pillows.

"Look at your sister."

"Mom, she didn't have to move to Maine to dress like a refugee from L.L. Bean catalogs."

"You're right," she said sadly.

"I'll tell you what," I said, choosing my words carefully. "If you ever die, I promise to establish a black checkpoint at the church door."

It wasn't clear if she was paying attention; or then again, I wasn't always sure if I was saying what I thought I was saying.

"In the old days I would never have gone to a funeral without a black lace mantilla over my head," she said. "Now there are some people who think that is excessive."

"Not on you, Mom. Never on you."

A few days later I went back to my doctor to have the staples removed. I'd had staples removed before, so I knew that
it was not entirely true what they told you, that it was painless. But it was better than setting off metal detectors forever
after. It was time for my body to hold itself together. Dr. von
Pfefferlingel was elegant in a blue suit, as always, and I was
embarrassed that he should have to deal with anything quite
so funky and visceral as these blood-and-pus-encrusted staples. God knows I would have liked to match his elegance, or
at least have black French underwear like my mother's.

He removed twenty-three staples. "I think we need to
count them again," I said. "I was dead set on twenty-two."
So Dr. von Pfefferlingel counted twenty-three, and Marie
the nurse counted twenty-three, and I counted twenty-
three small metal staples in the palm of my hand. "Where
was the twenty-third?" I asked. "

"Same place as the other twenty-two," said my doctor.

He asked me if I'd like to take them home, seeing as I had
no teratoma, in fact nothing except the scar to show for all
this trouble. I should have assured him that the scar would
be souvenir enough, but I could not bring myself to lie.

Traffic Court, or Ecumenical Outrage

"Your mother got another speeding ticket today," Gus said at dinner.

It was not as if I was not standing right there by the stove. I was. I was ladling tomato, mushroom, and olive sauce with more than a pinch of cumin onto heaps of lubricious vermicelli. For Cosmo I added five meatballs, arranged as the five points of a pentagram. For Gus and me, I made triangles. Cosmo had just waltzed in. Behind him, the kitchen door slammed shut like a meteorite hitting the Gobi Desert. How did he so consistently manage to achieve that resonance? He was returning from a game of basketball with his friends, which game he played every day after coming home from soccer practice and inhaling a large bowl of Cheerios. It has often been asked, but never satisfactorily answered: Before the advent of Cheerios, what did adolescent boys eat after their exertions? Was it porridge? Gruel? I have never seen the appeal of porridge, but then I've never liked Cheerios. It seems to be yet another way in which I am remiss in this arcane career of American motherhood, encumbered as it is by the need to know and recognize a thousand different cultural icons, television shows, baseball players, plastic toys that look like sexual aids and vice versa, packaged foods, wrestlers, and suicidal rock stars. More and more, it seems that I am my children's Community Service Project: Remedial Popular Culture 101, for our mother who knows the lives of the saints, Edith Piaf's songs, and the provenance of all the tropical fruits, but has never eaten a Krispy Kreme or seen *Friends*, or who just doesn't get it.

Cosmo was flushed red and handsome. His hands were damp enough to serve as a mycological breeding medium.

"Honey, you are seriously ripe. Could you please wash up before gracing the dinner table?" I said.

"Chill, Mom," Cosmo said. I knew I should be appalled by the rudeness, but I found his newfound minimalist vocabulary rather engaging: Chill, Phat with a PH, and Talk to the hand, The Face ain't Listening. Schooling, as in teaching with a vengeance. And Chief, always Chief. Of course, by the time I had mastered any idiom, it would have been already relegated to the dustbin of slang. It might even have become Correct Usage.

"Hey, Cos, did you hear about your mother's latest speeding ticket?" Gus said again.

"How did you know?" I said, suffused with fear, paranoia, nay terror.

I passed the salad bowl to Cosmo. I loved making salads, loved making a bed of greenery and then arranging hearts of palm or endives as spokes in the wheel, and then sprinkling it all with pine nuts or roofing it with pear slices so thin they were translucent.

"Mom, how many times have I explained to you the components of a normal salad: crunchy lettuce and tomatoes. This"—and Cosmo gestured extravagantly toward the beautiful heartwood bowl—"this looks like grass clippings and Amazonian insects."

"I like your mother's salads," Gus said.

"You know, it's a good thing I'm not sensitive about my culinary endeavors," I said. "Because if I were, I would be prostrate on the floor now, weeping uncontrollably, and swallowing arsenic."

"No, you wouldn't," Cosmo said. "Because that would emotionally scar me. And just the other day I heard you say that you were philosophically opposed to emotionally scarring one's children."

"Now, physical scarring is another matter," Gus said.

"Neither of you is funny," I said.

For a few seconds the only sound was the crunching and swallowing of food, and the stentorian snoring of Saint Joan under the table. But that would not last for long. Gus said again: "Your mother got another speeding ticket today."

"Could you please pass the meatballs?" Cosmo said.

"Did you hear about your mother?" Gus said.

"How many does that make, Mom?" It was obvious that all those amusing and even rhymed lessons I had taught him about the inadvisability of speaking with a mouthful of food had been forgotten. Or worse, were being wilfully ignored.

"Never mind," I said.

"I just wanted to know," said Cosmo.

"I'd like to know how *you* found out about it," I said to

Gus. I had this feeling of the porousness of my life, of the transparency of my emotions, of the pathetic obviousness of my intentions. It was all making me very nervous. I was at least ninety percent sure I had not told Gus about the speeding ticket. Did he have secret informers in the Crykskill Police Department? Unlikely. Was there a hidden bug in my car? Also unlikely. Was I being tailed by a sleazy man with a limp, a tic, and an overcoat? Was there a telltale look to one's car after being hailed by a siren? It would not do to become paranoid—I knew that.

"You told me when you got home," Gus said. "Don't you remember?"

"How can I remember something that didn't happen?" I said.

"How else would I know about it?" he said. "I'm not psychic."

"That's what I would like to know," I said. "I didn't say you were psychic."

"Please stop it, you guys. Mom, you were probably very upset and blurted it out and don't remember."

"He's right. And that's exactly how it happened. So will you tell us where you got it?" Gus said.

"Not in town," I said.

"Let's not turn this into Twenty Questions," Cosmo said.

"You used to love Twenty Questions," I said. "Back when you were a charming and compliant child who worshipped the ground his mother walked on."

"I'm still charming and I never worshipped dirt."

"It's an expression."

"Was it state or local police?" Gus said.

"Animal, vegetable, or mineral?" I said.

"The state police are the worst," Cosmo said. "They have NO sense of humor. I've heard that if they ever catch a trooper telling a joke, they throw him right off the force. It's just like mandatory sentencing."

"Do you remember the time on the Mass. Pike when the trooper wanted to take your father in for indecent exposure?" I said. This seemed a much more fruitful topic than my own recent traffic infraction.

"It was NOT indecent exposure," said Gus. "I was taking a whizz."

"I didn't say it was indecent, it was the cop. Remember? It was Christmas eve and we were going to your parents', or maybe my parents', and the cop said that you would ruin Christmas for all the innocent children driving by and seeing your Willie out there."

"He must have thought they traveled with binoculars," Cosmo said.

"I wasn't going to go there," I said.

Gus said, "It wasn't even the side of the road, I'd pulled off into that rest area just after the tollbooths. Your memory is a little faulty. And the trooper was a pervert as well as extremely aggressive."

"So did you threaten to sue him, Dad?"

"I didn't have to. I just asked for his name and mentioned I was a lawyer."

"You just mentioned it?"

Cosmo looked thoughtful and said, "Do you think lawyer

jokes are exempt from the Trooper's Humor Code? It's not as if they're funny."

"Are you going to tell us what you were stopped for?"

"You already know," I said. "Speeding. What else would it be? But the policeman seemed rather apologetic. He said he needed to stop someone because there had been complaints about that intersection, and that if I fight the ticket he promises not to be in court that day."

"So is that what you're going to do?"

"Of course. I don't want any more points on my license. Plus I've never been to Traffic Court, or any court. It might be interesting." Actually, I hadn't decided until that moment that I would fight the ticket, and now I feared that I had trapped myself in an indefensible position. What would I wear to Traffic Court? Wasn't I a bit old to be getting into these situations for which I had no instructions? Apparently not.

"What will you say to the judge?"

"I don't know. I guess I'll say I don't deserve a ticket."

"Why not?"

"Because I wasn't really going that fast."

"But you were speeding?"

"Whose side are you on, anyway?" I said. "I'm the injured party here."

"Not if you were speeding, you're not. You are aware, I assume, that you can't lie in court. That it's a bigger crime than speeding."

"Don't patronize me. Of course I know that."

Among the many things I had not considered was the problem of how to answer the question, Were you speeding or not? But maybe I would not be asked that question. Maybe when the policeman didn't show up the judge would send me home and apologize for wasting my time and then theatrically tear up the ticket.

The next night at dinner, I said to Gus and Cosmo, "Let's play Truth or Dare."

Cosmo's mouth and fingers were all engaged in what was for him the compelling task of removing every last bit of flesh from the tiny legs of the game hen, and so it was a moment or two before he said "Do you guys realize how pathetic it is the way we play these games at dinner?"

It was a rhetorical question. He was referring to Who Am I? and Botticelli, and the Capitals Game we'd played for years, thinking perhaps (and perhaps wrongly) that we were teaching our offspring the pleasures of dinner table conversation. But those games were what prepared Cosmo for that highlight of his Middle School career, when he made it to the Finals of the State Geography Championships. Those games were what prepared him to answer all those pertinent questions about the relative depths of the Great Lakes, and the language families in the Balkans, and the Roman names for all the Empire's outlying provinces, and the area in both square miles and square kilometers of all the South American countries. What is the largest living thing on the planet Earth? What is the Silk Road, and why?

So I had no intention of answering his question. Also, I forbore mentioning how loud was the crunching noise when he ate. What if I fed him ortolan? Bartavels? Partridges?

Wrens? Songbirds with tiny but deadly sharp beaks? Would the act of breaking their brittle bones with his teeth slow down the nightly barrage of humorous commentary?

"What I had in mind was a very specific Truth or Dare: Traffic Truth or Dare. Or if you prefer, Vehicular Truth or Dare."

Cosmo said, "Mom? Do you lie awake thinking up this stuff?"

"No, I dream it up. I don't need to be awake."

"So how do we play?"

"We take turns telling the worst thing we ever did in a car," I said. Across the table Gus's smile grew ominous. "Having to do with driving." My plate looked like the leavings of sloppy buzzards. I had never been good at sucking clean the bones of the various fowl we ate in this house.

"You mean like the time I drove the getaway car for the Post Office bombers," Cosmo said.

"Exactly, stuff like that."

"What a stupid idea," Gus said.

"It's a good idea," I insisted. I have to wonder now what I was thinking of. Was it some desired regression to the musky darkness of those confessionals in my youth? Contrary to all received wisdom, I had loved the simplicity of confession: the reduction of the chaotic sewage of the human mind into categorizable sins, the thoughts, the words, and the deeds, the venial and the mortal. The subsequent absolution and penance had been so easy. Too easy is what I think now, knowing as I do the mottled and rutted and stained and erased and restained condition of my soul.

I said to Gus and Cosmo, "I'll start. When I was sixteen and had just gotten my license, I drove to the Cape to see a friend and we smoked a joint and on the way home I hit every tree by the side of her driveway, which was a long dirt driveway. And I didn't even get out of the car to see. I just drove on home."

Gus rotated his index finger, like a bicycle wheel spinning without resistance.

"Now it's your turn," I said.

"Fine," he said. "Just to keep you happy. Once I drove all the way from the house to the Yacht Club using only my feet. My left foot did the brake and gas, and I steered with the toes on my right foot."

"I hope you washed your feet first," I said. "And the steering wheel after."

Cosmo pooh-poohed, "It's not even that far to the club."

"That's not the point," said Gus. "You try it. I know some Tantric yogis who couldn't manage it."

"Tantric yogis wouldn't be caught dead going to the Yacht Club."

"This is incredibly stupid," said Cosmo.

"That's been said before," I pointed out. "Now it's your turn, Cosmo. And it better not be too bad because you've only had your license for four months."

"You're censoring him already. That's an abrogation of his human rights."

"That's right. It's an aberration of my hoummus tights."

"Fine. Just forget it," I said. "Why don't we all just pout and watch *Jeopardy*."

"Chill, Mom," said Cosmo. "The first week I had my license and you guys let me drive the van to school, at lunchtime I drove all the kids on the team out to Mickey Dee's and someone who shall remain nameless threw his medium Coke into another car's open window on our way out of the lot."

"The Coke was that bad?" Gus said.

"That's awful, Cosmo," I said. "I mean, that is totally gratuitous violence, or vandalism, or hooliganism, or whatever you want to call it. Can you imagine how miserable I'd be to get into my car and find someone else's Coke all over the seat? I think I would cry." And I wanted to cry just then, for having stupidly started this, for the feeling that it was all slipping away too quickly, for that terrible unspeakable sense of loss. But I did not, because almost four years ago I had sworn to stop weeping at dinner, and for someone reason I had actually stuck to it.

"Mom, you asked for it."

"You were right. This is a stupid game," I said.

Gus said, "But I was just starting to enjoy it. Don't you want to hear about the time I was doing over a hundred in Nevada and actually took a turn on two wheels?"

"No."

"What about the time I got away from the trooper somewhere on the Maine Turnpike?"

"No. Just forget it. It was a really bad idea."

"No kidding," said Gus.

"Is there any more rice?" Cosmo asked.

"Loads," I said. "So what did you wear when you went to Traffic Court?"

"Who said I ever went to Traffic Court?"

"Just tell me what you wore. Because I know you did, and I even know why. Or just tell me what the women wore."

"G-strings? Overalls? I have no idea."

That night I sat in a dark room with only one reading lamp and looked at the portrait of Saint Teresa of Avila, the one painted by Juan de la Miseria when she was in her sixties and still quite attractive, and I noticed just how dark and bushy and prominent her eyebrows were. It was not Bernini's statue of Saint Teresa in ecstasy, being pierced with the arrow burning gold by the angel of God. It was not that Baroque erotic interpretation of Saint Teresa's raptures, the one that became the justification for all the later centuries' armchair diagnoses of her mental and sexual health. Not that one. In Juan de la Miseria's portrait—painted when the saint was still alive—Teresa is a competent and determined nun whose visions and levitations are safely private. Her hands are held in prayer and she is looking straight at the white dove. Her expression reminded me exactly of our Mother Superior at Saint Agatha's, Sister Seven Sorrows of Our Lady. Her expression could be translated as: *Do not even consider crossing me. I know what you are thinking before you think it.* Perhaps Sister Seven Sorrows modeled her daunting stare upon Saint Teresa's portrait. But Sister Seven Sorrows had no eyebrows, so the effect was very different.

That night, I realized just how easily the world could be divided into those with large eyebrows and those with thin or pale eyebrows. All my life, people had wanted to pluck my eyebrows, or so it had seemed to me. I had once let my mother give it a try, but as soon as I realized that the process involved actual pain, I fled and never again revisited the tweezers. Cosmo had large eyebrows like my father and brothers and me. But Gus had thin wispy eyebrows. Gus had once told me his eyebrows were so sparse because a gas oven had once exploded in front of him and burned off all his facial hair, and that had seemed a reasonable explanation for years, until it dawned on me that his siblings had equally sparse eyebrows. But what did it mean to have thick eyebrows? Was it simply a matter of genetics? When Rose, Gus's sister, dyed her eyebrows to make them darker and give them shape, her son had called her Groucho Marx. She'd spent the following week with her left hand covering her eyebrows, as if she was feeling especially thoughtful; the attempt was painfully obvious and highly comical, especially as she didn't look remotely like Groucho Marx. Saint Teresa looked more like Groucho Marx than Rose ever did.

The next night there was a strange unseasonable storm brewing. The sky was as shiny gray as a new frying pan and the air felt dangerous and otherworldly.

I said, "You know what seems a shame about spring thunderstorms?"

"They ruin my lettuce seedlings?" Gus said.

"Wrong," I said.

"Not wrong," said Gus. "Perhaps not what you were thinking of, but not wrong."

"Whatever," I said, and made a **W** by touching the tips of my thumbs to each other and opening up the slope between the index finger and thumb of each hand. I had just learned this semaphore from one of Cosmo's girlfriends, and I was pleased with it.

"You just don't like vegetables. You've never eaten enough vegetables."

"Just because I'm not a rabbit doesn't mean I don't eat enough vegetables."

"Mom, your ears are too small for even a baby rabbit."

"Thanks, Cosmo. Was that a compliment? "

"We haven't eaten rabbit around here in ages. I liked those rabbits we had in France. Can you cook up some bunnies sometime soon, Mom?"

I said, "Can we just finish with this thunderstorm?"

"What thunderstorm?"

"The one that is hovering on the horizon as we speak. The one whose electricity is making Saint Joan shake like a demented limbo dancer. That storm," I shouted.

"What about it?" Gus said.

"Just that it seems a shame they don't get named."

"That's because it's not a hurricane. Only hurricanes get names."

"Not so," I said. "What about tropical storms? Tropical storm Sally, or George? Although I hate it when they get male names. I much preferred the old days when all the hurricanes were female. Like Hindu goddesses."

"What do Hindu goddesses have to do with it?" Cosmo asked.

"Early onset of Alzheimer's," Gus explained.

"The Hindus understand the connection between

destruction and creativity. The powers thereby unleashed.
What's-her-name, the destroyer goddess. And I should point
out that it is tacky to make Alzheimer cracks to someone
whose best-beloved Bonne Maman has it."

"She is my great-grandmother," Cosmo said. "But I'm not
sensitive about Alzheimer's."

"You're sixteen, not forty-six, or eighty-six," I pointed out.

"You're thinking of Shiva, and he's a god," Gus said.

"Well, there's another one who's a goddess. Besides, the
Hindus aren't so absolutist about what sex you are," I
pointed out.

"In which case it should be all right to give hurricanes
names of any gender."

"Except that we aren't Hindus. They have monsoons and
I don't know what they name them. We have need of other
nomenclature."

"Other what?" Cosmo said.

"Kali!" I said. "Kali was the destroyer. She has multiple
arms and breathes fire, or drips blood, or something along
those lines."

"I know about Kali," said Gus. "She's just an incarnation
of Shiva, also his wife."

"I would love the job of naming the hurricanes," I said.
And it was true. I was always renaming the hurricanes so designated by the National Hurricane Center, naming them for
early saints, generally martyrs. Arnie became Angadrisima,
of whom it is said that she "asked God to make her so physically repulsive as to put marriage out of the question, and
she was accordingly visited with leprosy." In my personal

meteorological hagiography, Mitch became Magdalena and Hugo became Hildegund, one of the cross-dressing saints, and Oscar became Opportuna, virgin and martyr, and Stan became Solangia, one of the legendary cephalophores.

I told them, "One of my favorite things about being pregnant was thinking up names for the baby."

"And you came up with Cosmo?"

"I love the name Cosmo. If you'd had a twin he could have been Damien. The surgical wonders to behold. But I like Cosmo the best, although I was torn between that and Orlando, and Boniface." Years ago I had heard, though from a source I have since been unable to rediscover, that Cosmas and Damien, early Christian twin doctor saints, were famous in their time for grafting a leg onto an amputee. It was a black leg onto a white stump. Such apocrypha were not to be found in Butler's nor in any other hagiography in my library. In which case, where?

"I'll never complain about Cosmo again," Cosmo said.

"Of course not," I said. "It's a lovely name. When your father first started his campaign to call Winnie Winifred, for his Grangran, I was seriously worried, on account of Saint Winifred, whose head was chopped off by an irate suitor. So it seemed somewhat risky to me."

"Riskier than Cosmo?"

"But her uncle Saint Bueno popped it right it back on and so Winifred lived a long and nunnical life."

"What a relief," Cosmo said.

"The point is," I said. "That you both have lovely names."

• • •

Given that I knew I was a better and safer driver than any of the males in the family, it seemed unfair to me that I was the one who had been getting speeding tickets of late. Not that I was in danger of having my license suspended, not yet. That would require eleven points in eighteen months, which would call for more than three violations (worth three points each) of ten miles per hour over the speed limit, or two violations (worth six points each) of twenty to thirty miles over the limit, or just one violation (worth eleven points) of more than forty miles over the limit, which even in my most panicked or daring moments I am certain I have never achieved.

The most recent insult before the current ticket had been acquired while driving north with my friend Tippit to see her friend the yoga instructor and natural healer. I recall that I was slightly exasperated with Tippit because she wouldn't say whether or not she was sleeping with Phil, the yoga instructor and natural healer. I knew I shouldn't let it get to me, because she was English and pathologically incapable of making simple declarative sentences. So I undertook to clarify for her this personality quirk, as well as explain how it was deeply rooted in her weird English family and their moldy manor house in Dorset or Derbyshire and all the relatives with skeletal secrets, and how they were now supporting a good portion of the psychiatric population of the Western world. Which money, I pointed out, if they could only learn to speak those declarative sentences I was so fond of, they could save up and put into central heating.

When the siren sounded, I assumed it was another overweening and humorless trooper and that his car would quickly pass me and go on to terrorize some other innocent driver. So it was a shock when the flashing lights stayed right behind me and I realized that the siren was bellowing for me. I'd been doing eighty-five in a sixty-five-mile-per-hour zone, which if this had taken place in New York would have added four points to my license. But happily we were not in New York. Not that I knew it at the time. I thought we were still in New York when he pulled me over, and so in the interval between the stopping and the appearance of the trooper at my window, I heaped verbal abuse on the morals, personal hygiene, and intelligence of New York State Troopers, when I should have been directing my invective at Mainers.

But that was then, and now I was summoned to appear in Traffic Court in Crykskill to defend my claim of being not guilty of speeding, specifically of going fifty-eight miles per hour in a thirty-mile-per-hour zone (six-point offense). And I was guilty, though perhaps not as guilty as twenty-eight miles over the limit. And I had no idea what one wore to traffic court. Being guilty added to my consternation about what to wear. What did I own that looked not only Not Guilty, but Appropriately Humble in the eyes of the law? I had several lovely and well-cut suits, all in various shades of gray and black, not including summer suits of ecru, ivory, and pale seaweed, but as it was still before Memorial Day, they were a nonissue. Yet I suspected that all those suits would be more than a little too well-cut for the Crykskill Traffic Court and I might be accused of looking like an upper-middle-class, middle-aged suburban matron, which of course I was. But I couldn't help that.

The speeding ticket before the one with Tippit in Maine was the direct result of my righteous indignation regarding the acronym for a delivery company. Imagine that you are peaceably driving down the highway, singing along with the Rolling Stones, or quizzing your children as to the life plans of every single classmate of theirs, based on SAT scores and college applications, and you look in the rearview mirror and see that a fourteen-and-a-half-ton truck is glommed onto your rear bumper like an Okefenokee leech. Calmly, peaceably, with only the mildest of uttered expletives, you move into the right lane so that the pursuing behemoth can pass you, and as he does so you read this on the side of the truck: G.O.D. You look again and see that these letters purport to stand for Guaranteed Overnight Delivery. And you are outraged.

Or I was outraged.

"Can you believe the hubris?" I said to my family.

"What is Mom talking about?" Winnie said. Perhaps we were all driving Winnie up to college, or else heading north for one of those massive family birthday or anniversary parties. It was not a funeral; I do not get confused about funerals, although even then I frequently speed, but with a great sense of the exigencies and entitlement of mourning. It was always more fun when Winnie was in the car along with Cosmo, because then they annoyed and amused each other in that secret sibling way they have. And I was left to daydream and speed while Gus did the crossword puzzle: the *Times* Saturday crossword, the only one difficult enough to be worth his while.

"Just read the side of that truck," I instructed them.

"I get it," said Cosmo. "She's talking about the God."

"I'm talking about the outrageous gall of some avaricious heathen in giving his company that name, and thinking he is actually clever."

"You assume it's a guy," Gus said.

"Of course. No woman would be so blasphemous, or so obvious."

"Don't you think you're overreacting?" Winnie said.

"No, I don't," I said. "I think it's important that we get incensed by flagrant blasphemy. I think outrage is healthy."

"Why shouldn't a trucking company use that name? Do you think Catholics have a lock on calling God God?" Gus said.

"Did I say it has anything to do with Catholics? Did I? I think this is a case for ecumenical outrage," I said.

"Are you sure you saw it right?" Cosmo said. The truck was now at least five lengths ahead of us, in the middle lane. "Come on, catch up with him. I want to see the great outrage."

"Your mother should have been a Grand Inquisitor," Gus said.

"Not all Inquisitors were evil, you know," I said. "Many of them had the best intentions. Things just got a little out of hand in Spain and a few other places."

Who knows to what nadirs this discourse might have descended, had we not been interrupted. I did as requested and pressed the accelerator and came alongside the offensive truck, the perpetrator of outrage, so that Gus and Winnie and Cosmo and even Saint Joan, if she was so moved, could appreciate the outrage. By then I was going about eighty miles per hour, which gives you an idea of how fast the truck was going if I had to go eighty in order to just come along beside it. So when I heard the siren I did not immediately assume it was for me. The G.O.D. truck seemed a far more likely candidate for the attentions of our state constabulary. But then it became clear that the siren was for me, and my righteous indignation blossomed to such vast proportions that I pictured it filling the car and then leaking out the windows and engulfing the surrounding highways.

"Oh, Mom, not again," said Cosmo.

"Not one bloody word from you," I said, pulling onto the shoulder. "This is a case of persecution."

"Are you sure you want to go there?" Gus said.

"Do you want to trade places? Honestly, it's okay with me if you want this ticket."

The policeman walked up to my window with that perfect lack of expression that recalls Noh theatre. He looked in at Gus and Cosmo and Winnie and Saint Joan and me, impassive. It's funny how I persisted in thinking that no policeman would ever want to give a ticket to a mother with two such lovely children and especially with such an expressive and lugubrious bulldog. Yet not once had I succeeded in getting out of a ticket on the basis of my nuclear family. Delusions persist: that is the nature of delusions.

He asked for my license and registration, which I handed over with alacrity.

"Before you go back and check the computer," I said. "You might want to also check on that truck that was beside me. He was going much faster because in fact I never even passed him."

"Is that what you were trying to do?" The policeman said.

"Well, in fact I was really trying to get beside him so my children could see the name of the company, because I was so upset that a company would call itself G.O.D." I didn't say *God*. I spelled it out, to make my point.

"I don't see how that matters. I clocked you going eighty-two, Ma'am."

"Well, yes," I said. "But that was because I wanted my children to read the side of the truck, because I don't think an ordinary delivery company should call itself G.O.D. even as an acronym. Besides, I can't believe I was going that fast."

"Are you questioning the accuracy of my radar?"

"I don't know anything about your radar," I said.

"My radar clocked you at eighty-two," he said.

"Be that as it may," I said. "I'm just pointing out that the truck, which is now long gone, was going even faster."

"You're welcome to contest the ticket, lady." I noticed that I was no longer Ma'am.

Gus was starting to emit a low growl in the seat beside me. "Just be quiet," he said.

"How do I contest the ticket?" I asked.

"Just follow the instructions, lady," the policeman said. "But you should know that I'm certified in six different types of radar, at the widest range of speeds."

"Oh," I said.

So he went back to his cop car and we sat in our car waiting while he checked with some central computer to

find out if I was an escaped felon or an embezzler or an at-
large Belgian terrorist. When the trooper had been gone for
at least a whole three minutes, Gus said, "Jesus fucking
Christ." And then we sank into silence again. A few minutes
later the cop came back to my window and handed me the
ticket. About ten miles later I pulled over so that Gus could
drive, because I was not one bit less outraged by the blasphemy of Guaranteed Overnight Delivery.

I could have thought about it for another decade and I still
would have worn the wrong thing to Traffic Court. In my
gray pleated skirt and white linen blouse and mustard cash-
mere sweater I looked like a prewar headmistress. Before we
had finished going through security, I knew how wrong it
was. The guards at security took away my water bottle, and
my knitting scissors and crochet hook, but they left me the
size ten circular needles I was using to make an excruciat-
ingly soft (because of the angora) mauve baby bunting for
Tippit's long-awaited infant.

On the summons, it said to appear in Traffic Court at
eleven A.M., and I was there at ten-fifty-five. I'd wanted to
give myself enough time to find the place, if it was hard to
find, if there was some Kafkaesque architecture to be negoti-
ated. But I hadn't wanted to get there too early, because that
might seem overeager, might seem Guilty with a capital G.
Traffic Court was on the third floor and when I got there I
found many other people waiting to enter; it turned out
that they too had been told to arrive at eleven A.M. It was
dawning on me that Traffic Court was not like having an

appointment with my gynecologist, who would apologize if he was five minutes late for an eleven o'clock appointment. More and more people with similar eleven A.M. summonses wandered into the hallway outside the room marked "Traffic Court." There was not a single chair or bench available for the waiters. A woman in tight leopard-print pants went back and forth across the hall, swinging on her aluminum crutches; when it became painfully obvious that no respite would appear, she sighed and leaned against a post. This chairlessness struck me as the height of bureaucratic inconsideration, if not actual intimidation. I very much minded not having a chair to offer her. I thought of those clever three-legged folding stools that I often admired—and even briefly considered purchasing—in catalogs. They were usually photographed beneath the posterior of an elegant lady, herself beneath a large-brimmed hat, at an event that was supposed to look like the races at Saratoga. But even if I had brought such a clever folding stool with me, which I might have, if I owned one and if I had known about the lack of chairs in the hallway, the security guards would probably have taken it away. For reasons of their very own.

I watched as various policemen approached and spoke with several persons who appeared to be waiting for Traffic Court. No one approached me.

After many minutes, the door to the room labeled "Traffic Court" was opened and people who clearly knew what they were doing started going in and seating themselves. I followed them. I sat down, and read for the hundredth time the instructions on my summons. I was too

nervous to read Rousseau's *Confessions,* which I had in my
purse along with my knitting and the Arts section of the
Times. The crossword puzzle seemed to be the best way to
keep myself from perspiring. Knitting with sweaty hands
was not a good idea. *Icelandic literary output:* eddas; *Ulan—:*
Bator; *Ankara small change:* lira; *Many a snake:* hisser. Those were
the easy ones; those were the clues that sucked me in and
then when I realized that all the long answers were related
to country music singers and songs, I knew it was hopeless
that I would ever complete the puzzle and that I should
have stuck with my knitting. By then it was too late.

The traffic judge came in while I was grappling with this
clue: *Part of an impolite word?* Someone shouted incoherently
and we all stood up. Wasn't this what they did in real court-
rooms? And all I had done was drive too fast. I became posi-
tively diaphoretic, which would have been a fair clue for
sweaty. We sat down.

There was a bailiff calling out names, and then individuals
approached the bench—as they say—and a whole gamut of
traffic violations was dealt with: speeding a little, running a
red light, speeding a lot, driving to endanger, speeding.
There was no obvious order in which people were called; I
could only determine orders in which they were not called:
not alphabetical; not chronologically by date of infraction;
not by age (this only a guess, but it seemed safe); not reverse
alphabetical. Which meant that I could not anticipate when
I would be called to the bench, which uncertainty only
increased my diaphoresis.

Asterisk. The answer was asterisk.

Nor was there an obvious pattern to the judgments being passed down. Some violators were fined, whether or not the ticketing officer was present. Others were dismissed. In one hotly contested case where the ticketed young woman claimed that the trooper had mistaken her car for another that had taken the exit, judgment was postponed for further deliberations, though what those entailed was in no way explained. I wanted a pattern.

Then my name was called; as usual it was slightly mispronounced. I looked around the room just to see if anyone else was moving, on the chance that it was not my name mispronounced but someone else's name pronounced correctly, as in Ur-soo-la Ox-eree Codwell, but no one was moving.

So I placed the newspaper, crossword facing down, beside me on the bench. And I went forward. As soon as the judge addressed me, I was assaulted with the realization that I had been there before. I saw the whole scene: The judge, with his bushy volcanic eyebrows which were just like Saint Teresa of Avila's eyebrows in the portrait by Juan de la Miseria only more so; myself in this particular pleated skirt, which was like the uniforms at every Catholic school except the one I attended thirty-five or so years ago; the compelling ringing in my ears and the attendant desire to ream them out past the auricular concha all the way into the acoustic meatus and remove all the years of accumulated cerumen, and the imperative of not sticking my fingers in my ears but keeping them down below my waist. I prayed for the weight of gravity to keep them down there, even as it seemed that this natural law had been reversed and something was tugging at my fingers, like marionette strings, pulling them earward. *Tinnitus, tinnitus,* I kept thinking, and realizing at the same time that this had all happened before, even to being unable to stop silently chanting that word: *tinnitus. tinnitus. tinnitus. tinnitus.* It resonated like a mantra in my yoga class. For its trance-inducing properties, it was better than Hindi.

But I had not been to Traffic Court before. Never. Not in all my years of speeding. So this was just a déjà vu. It was that simple. It wasn't simple at all. Not for me it wasn't.

Either I had been here before, or I had been in some similar parallel universe (which was the sort of scientific concept that tied me in knots), or it was all an illusion. I wondered if the judge with the eyebrows of Saint Teresa ever broke through the tedium of fining and sentencing and dismissing, to feel that he'd done it all before. Or not.

With the greatest of effort, I kept my fingers out of my ears, kept them from probing all the way to my cochlear fenestra. Kept myself from giving more than a passing thought to the window to the snail inside my ear. The judge with the volcanic eyebrows pointed out that since the ticketing officer was not present he would dismiss my case, unless I had any objections. Did this require a response on my part? Maybe I whispered my thanks to the judge, or maybe I did not actually contrive to make a sound. And then I collected the crossword puzzle and my knitting and Rousseau's *Confessions,* and left the Traffic Courtroom.

"I have an announcement," I said at dinner. No one stopped eating, eyelids barely flickered. Such, I suppose, could be attributed to the compelling flavors of palmito lasagna and passion-fruit sorbet with cherimoya. Or such could be the exigencies of hunger. "I never sped on March fifteenth on Route 9. Any record of a speeding ticket has been expunged from my record. The marriage of Traffic Violation and yours truly has been annulled. Justice has been served. My license is now point-less."

"I get it," said Cosmo.

Gus said, "Let me get this straight. You were speeding. You got a ticket. You show up in court. The judge dismisses the case."

"That's one way of putting it," I said. "But I prefer my gloss on events."

"You always do," Gus said.

"It was the least they could do after I got all dressed up and suffered centuries of anxiety and imagined myself on Devil's Island with only rats and spiders for company. The very least."

Gus said, "It's not the DMV's problem that you're hysterical."

"Hyperbolical," Cosmo said.

"Yes," I said. "But then I make the rest of you look so reasonable."

"Hyperbole, synecdoche, zeugma, and . . . what was that last one? And what is this?" Cupped in his left hand like a piece of dangerous, or breakable, porcelain, was a hemisphere of cherimoya.

"That," I said happily. "That is a cherimoya. The queen of tropical fruits. Finding cherimoya in this clime is the happy end of a long quest."

"This flesh is too white," Cosmo said. "Kind of like larvae."

"Close your eyes when you taste it," Gus said.

"Not bad," Cosmo said.

Gus said, "He has determined that the queen of tropical fruits is *pas mal*."

I spooned out the white flesh and dark seeds of cherimoya, and placed them in my mouth. And then I thought that surely this absolutely perfect fruit, perfectly sweet but not too sweet, perfectly soft without being mushy, also called a custard apple, was the fruit that had been irresistible to Eve and Adam in their paradisiacal first home. This idea struck me with the sudden clarity of a thunderbolt. It was as if I'd found a long-lost manuscript with instructions for finding true love or never ever getting cavities.

"I just had an epiphany," I said to Gus and Cosmo.

"Let me guess," Gus said. "It's food-related."

"Do you know what else cherimoya are called? In English, that is?"

"Slimy?" Cosmo suggested.

"No. They're called custard apples." I spoke slowly, hoping for maximum effect. It seems I hoped in vain.

"I always thought custard apples were cow dung," Cosmo said.

"You're thinking of prairie apples. At least I think they call them prairie apples. It's been a while since I've ridden the prairie."

"I can't wait to hear this," Gus said.

"Cherimoya was the fruit in the Garden of Eden. No, wait: think about it. It's tropical. It's unbelievably delicious. But it's kind of secret, with that greenish hard skin giving no clue to what's inside. Like knowledge."

"I told you that years ago. Don't you remember? The first time we ate it in Costa Rica? I told you how scholars have determined the location of Eden in Sri Lanka, and proposed cherimoya as one, ONE, of the possible contenders for the killer fruit."

"You never told me that," I said.

Gus said, "You just don't remember. You only remember what suits you."

"I have homework," Cosmo said. He carried the remains of his meal over to the kitchen counter, and headed upstairs. It was probably time for *The Simpsons*, without which he could not concentrate on the Uncertainty Principle or the medieval guild system.

"How sad," I said. "And I thought I'd had this great revelation which would be of great benefit to mankind."

"How would that be of great benefit to mankind?"

"Because everyone has been longing to know exactly which fruit it was back in Eden, and now they would know."

"That's assuming a) you're a creationist, and b) that you accept the choice of cherimoya, and c) that we didn't already know about custard apples, and d) . . . well, forget about d)."

"This is upsetting me terribly," I said. "It if were not for the happy—and APPROPRIATE—outcome of Traffic Court, I think I would be prostate with grief."

"Prostrate," Gus said.

"I still don't think you ever told me about that. We hadn't even tasted cherimoya until about five years ago."

"Wrong," Gus said.

Before going to Traffic Court I had not known, not in the premier vu or the déjà vu, that the judge's eyebrows could have been made of mouse skin. Not that it was likely. But in previous times, up to and around the eighteenth century, artificial eyebrows were made of mouse skin, and certainly Saint Teresa's eyebrows could have been made of mouse skin, had she been inclined to beauty aids. It was better that I did not know this while I was in Traffic Court.

Had I told Gus about my theory of eyebrows? I was absolutely sure I had not. Because I could think of all the people whose eyebrows were neither thick nor thin, and it became obvious that this was yet another attempt at organizing and explaining the world that would not work.

Why the French?

ate in the afternoon, I picked up Cosmo after his
track meet. It was almost dark out, almost nightfall.
But already it was less dark than it had been this time
of day a month ago, already it was less dark than the darkness that leads up to the winter solstice, that deep darkness
at the end of Advent.

"How did you run?" I asked him. Or maybe what I said
was, What did you run?

"The mile," he said.

In the afternoons, Cosmo's conversation tends towards
the monosyllabic. It always amazes me how, when one really
tries, much of life can be expressed in fewer than twenty-five
English words, mostly of Anglo–Saxon origin. Of course I
long for more details, for longer, Latinate words and deeply
felt expressions, but I can just keep on longing in vain, faced
as I am with the implacable and hulking silence of Cosmo, a
boy not quite a man, but very close.

"How long was the mile?" I asked, and quickly regretted
it. "I mean, how fast did you run?"

"Not fast enough."

"OK, but is there a number attached to that phrase?" I said.

"Four fifty-two," he said.

"You mean four minutes and fifty-two seconds?" I said, with muted admiration, careful not to jump for maternal pride.

"No, I mean four light years and fifty-two decades," Cosmo said.

"I'm not a complete idiot, you know," I said. To which he replied not at all. "That sounds like an excellent time to me," I said. "It's a lot faster than I've ever run a mile."

"That's not saying much, Mom," he said.

"I know that; I'm just trying to express my admiration for your fleetness of foot. Speaking of which, do you know what a mile comes from?"

"I know how many feet are in a mile, if that's what you mean."

"Actually," I said, "I was referring to its etymology, from the Latin for thousand, *millia,* and also the French, *mille,* because in Roman times a mile was a thousand paces."

"Fascinating," said Cosmo.

"Well, it is," I said. "When you consider that there aren't a thousand of anything in the mile anymore. Not a thousand feet, or yards, or . . . "

"I get it, Mom."

"I just think the various standards of measure around the world are incredible. Did you know that the Scottish mile used to be about two hundred feet longer than the English, and the Irish still use a different mile? Think how difficult it is to accurately compare speed or anything from one place to another."

"That's why we mostly do things in meters," said Cosmo.

"But not everything. In Costa Rica we still use manzanas for coffee farms, so when we want to compare our yield per manzana with yields in any other country, where they mostly use hectares, we have to do lots of math. Which as you know can be a problem for yours truly."

"Mom!" Cosmo sputtered. "Did you go to the bank today?"

"Oh, yes," I said. I had been waiting for this. "About your ATM card. I got it for you, but it has to be in my name because you're not eighteen yet."

"That is the most outrageous rule I've ever heard," he said. Cosmo's capacity for indignation has always been vast.

"It's not worth losing sleep over," I said.

He said, "Principles are always worth losing sleep over." Then he lowered his window and spit out a dozen orange pips; he must have been saving them in some recess of his mouth the entire time he was peeling and sectioning and eating his orange, and throughout our entire conversation.

"And one more thing. I forgot your PIN so I had to make one up for you on the spot," I said.

"How could you forget?"

"Easily," I said. "That's why everyone uses their birthdays."

"That's ridiculous," said Cosmo. "So what is the PIN?"

"1431."

"1431? Where did you get that?"

"It was the first thing that came into my head," I told him.

"The first thing that came into your head? Does it mean anything?"

"Actually," I said, and I knew I was skating on thin ice. I was entering the red zone. "It means a couple of things."

"Such as?"

"Well, it's the year Joan of Arc was burned at the stake."

There was a little explosion in the front seat, a kind of contained volcanic eruption. "Mom! You know I can't abide this Joan of Arc shit."

"Remember we're having a moratorium on the *merde* word," I said.

"I can't believe you put that number in. This really pisses me off."

"Don't think about poor Joan then. Only nineteen and they burned her. But if you can't find it in your heart to think of her and her courage, then think about François Villon."

"What about that froggy Villon?"

"He was born in 1431. The saint dies and the sinner is born. Kind of a Dostoyevskian synergy, if you look at it that way."

Cosmo was moaning. He'd really loved *Crime and Punishment,* so I was hoping to win him over with this observation. Of course I would fail.

Cosmo and his uncle had been amusing themselves at my expense since a certain Sunday dinner a month before. My nephew Cato, who went to art school in the city and came up to us on Sundays to feed at the trough, brought with him a certain Allegra from Barnard, whom he described as a "potential" girlfriend. She said she was a French major and so I asked her how she liked François Villon, and she said she didn't know who he was. I suggested that she quickly make his acquaintance if she planned on getting anywhere in the study of French literature. At which point Dennis, my Philistine brother-in-law—the one obsessed with feminine hygiene products—proceeded to mock me and revile François Villon, whom he kept referring to, on purpose, as Jean-Claude.

I am not being nasty when I label Dennis as a Philistine; it is a rubric he aspires to. He does not know, nor does he want to know, that Saint Denis—for whom he was surely not named, Unitarians being strangers to the wise tradition of naming one's children for saints—is the patron saint of France. I would wager a lifetime supply of fine French wine (which in Dennis's case would be around 13,505 bottles or 1,125 and a half cases, a number arrived at by multiplying the number of remaining years he has, based on the statistical life span of a white male in his income bracket, by the number of days in a year, 365) that he knows nothing at all of the controversy surrounding the true identity of Saint Denis—he whose beheaded body was retrieved from the Seine, honorably buried and later served as the foundation for the chapel around which rose the great abbey of Saint Denis. You can take it for a fact that my brother-in-law Dennis cares not a whit whether Saint Denis, the third-century Bishop of Paris, and Saint Denis the Areopagite, who was congenial with Saint Paul in the first century, were the same person.

This is what really happened:

I was serving poached salmon that Sunday for our dinner; I make it my mother's way, with buttered leeks and white wine, and it is generally considered quite good. My mother refers to this as the Belgian way, Saumone à la Belge or some such nonsense, but given that she never inhabited Belgium past her first month of life, I think that attribution is her fantasy.

So there we were, sitting down for Sunday dinner, and I asked Allegra what she was studying, and she said she'd just decided to major in French literature.

"Great," I said. I was truly delighted. To have another Francophile at the table would be a new delight. For men who imbibed such vast quantities of Merlot and Medoc and Armagnac, my husband Gus and his brother Dennis were inexplicably unrepentant Francophobes; they blamed their inability to speak or understand the French language on the intransigence of the Gallic character, rather than on their own flat ears and smug parochialism. So there was Allegra, young and obviously untainted by this Americansky xenophobia. I instantly planned for her to have a long and satisfying relationship with Cato, which would include many Sunday dinners when we would all happily discuss Mauriac, Molière, Rimbaud, and Colette, maybe hum a few bars of Gounod and Edith Piaf; there were all sorts of possibilities, and none of them included the Patriots or professional wrestling. I said, "So you must be reading some François Villon."

"No, I don't think so," she said.

"But you're planning to?" I asked. I was pleased to be managing to serve up the salmon with so very few bones, and almost not using my fingers at all. Although it was becoming clear that for Cosmo and Cato this poisson was more of an entr'acte and once again, mere minutes after they had eaten what I considered a complete Sunday dinner, they would be at the kitchen table scarfing up bowls of Cheerios.

"I don't know," she said. "I've never heard of him."

"François Villon! Well, you're in for a treat," I said. I thought it was obvious that I wasn't trying to embarrass her, merely to educate, elucidate, expatiate, illuminate.

"Shocking!" said Dennis, in his best Queen of England accent. "This poor child hasn't read Jean-Claude Vertigo. I assume you'll be dropping out of school next week."

"You're an idiot, Dennis," I said. "It's François and I didn't say she had to have already read it, just to look forward to it."

"I'm sure she can't wait," he said.

"Just because your cultural education stopped with the Three Stooges doesn't mean that everyone else wants to stay developmentally arrested. This charming young lady, for instance," I said.

Cato seemed to find this mildly amusing.

"He was one of the first poets to write in the French vernacular—in the fifteenth century," I said. "He was a wild young student, constantly getting himself into trouble for hanging priests in effigy and things like that."

"They hanged him in the end," Gus addressed Allegra.

"Actually not," I said. "No one knows how he died because he was exiled from Paris and never heard of again."

"Not so," said Gus. "He was convicted of several crimes, but they hanged him for the last one."

"They can't have hanged him," I said. I was as sure of this as I could be, as sure as I was of how Virginia Woolf had drowned and Joan of Arc had burned, but still, something was making me nervous. "Because the whole point is that no one knows how he died. Once he left Paris he was never heard from again. Exile from Paris was the worst thing that could happen back then," I said. "*Mais ou sont les neiges d'antan?* Maybe it still is."

Gus said, "The whole point of what?"

"Of the story."

"Paris is full of the French," Dennis slurred in his faux French accent.

"I know," I said. "That's just one of the great things about it."

"And Villon was hanged in Paris," Gus insisted.

"No, he wasn't." I said. "I happen to know this. I read him in French for one thing." As soon as I said this I knew it was a mistake; Dennis, for one, would never let me live it down, and Gus didn't like being contradicted about facts.

"Très bien," Dennis said. "Quelle accomplishment. Because the Jean-Claude Virus I know wrote in pig-Latin. So reading him in French must have been très difficult."

"You're not funny, Dennis," I said.

"Your son thinks I am," he said.

"He also watches *The Simpsons.* He still makes bathroom jokes," I pointed out.

"How versatile! And what *is* wrong with bathroom jokes?" Dennis asked.

"Maybe it's time we talked about something else." I said. "Something simple, like religion or politics."

Gus said, "He even wrote a Last Will or testament, before he was hanged."

"When he was in his twenties he wrote his Legacy, *Le Lais,* where he bequeaths things—like his dogs and his gloves and his heart in a casket, and bundles of straw and naked children—to various characters. That must be what you're thinking of."

"You have no idea what I'm thinking of," Gus said.

"You're right," I said. "I have no idea what you're thinking of because I know he was not hanged."

"You're being obtuse," Gus said.

"Obtuse? Are you sure you don't mean abstruse? Or obscure?" Gus was not finding me amusing.

"Or you could be confusing that with *Le Testament*, which he wrote when he was about thirty, a mere couple of years before he disappeared from literary history," I insisted. "But he was never hanged. Shall I get the encyclopedia? Or the Larousse?"

Allegra, she whose education we were all so incensed about, looked over at Cato as if to ask if this behavior was normal. Cato stopped chewing long enough to say, "Someone can always kiss it good-bye when they bring out the encyclopedia."

"Or the dictionary," said Dennis. "I bet Jean-Claude Virus never read the dictionary for amusement."

Gus glared at me over the shimmering glassware and the empty serving dishes and the guttering candles, and said "Then you can prepare to kiss it good-bye. He was hanged."

"Very funny, Dad," Cosmo said.

I produced the fifteenth edition of the Encyclopedia Britannica, Volume 19, Utilitarianism to Zwingli, and I read, not without a certain pleasure: "After his banishment by the Parlement of 1463 all trace of Villon is lost."

"That doesn't say he was not hanged," Gus said.

I flourished another volume, Wyndham Lewis's biography,

the one with the peculiar typeface that binds all the *st*'s with a ligature in the shape of an umbrella. "I have here the pertinent chronology. And I quote:

> *"1462—Villon returns to Paris. November 3–7: Villon imprisoned in the Châtelet and released on a bond to the Faculty of Theology. Villon implicated in the stabbing of Master François Ferrebourg, re-arrested, and sentenced to be hanged and strangled. 1463, January 3: Parliament, on Villon's appeal, commutes the death sentence to banishment for ten years. Villon vanishes from history."*

"He was condemned to die—to be hanged," Gus repeated.

"But the sentence was commuted. Are you paying attention? I'm the one who speaks French here," I said.

"I think it's time we got another encyclopedia. When was that book published, anyway? It's very possible that I am in possession of new information," Gus said.

"Possible, but not likely," I said.

"This salmon is delicious," my sister-in-law said. "Where did you get it?"

"The Korean grocers," I told her.

"They have the best fish," she said.

I turned to Allegra. "So, what other writers will you be studying? And please don't pay attention to them."

She looked at me with something akin to horror and chewed her food very slowly. Perhaps, like me, she had been taught to chew each morsel ten times. In addition, Bonne Maman, my maternal grandmother, instructed me—in French, her mother tongue—to run my tongue around the perimeter of my mouth ten times clockwise, and then ten times counterclockwise, before speaking in anger. Would that I had.

Since that dinner of leeks and fishes, whenever it is deemed amusing by Gus or Cosmo or Dennis to call attention to my nerdiness, or my general unconnectedness to the so-called "real" world of insurance, competitive sports, and socialized medicine, reference is made to the time I humiliated this poor Barnard girl by demanding that she recite Jean-Claude Viridium, all of which is totally untrue.

She was never humiliated. She appreciated my advice. His name was never Jean-Claude, and she really should know his poetry.

"What made you think I'd want Frank Villon's birthday as my PIN?" Cosmo asked.

"I didn't think you would. It was just the first number that came to mind and I knew I wouldn't forget it before I saw you."

"But I can't stand the guy," Cosmo said.

"You're just saying that because Dennis and your dad have irrational prejudices against the French. How can you not stand someone you don't even know?" I asked.

"I know he's French and he's dead."

"That's a big chunk of humanity you're condemning there," I pointed out. "What about Baudelaire? He's French and dead. But your sister loves him."

"She also loves David Bowie. She would marry David Bowie if he were not a freak of nature."

"But you would have liked Villon if you'd just give him a chance. He was an anarchic and brilliant student and poet. He was the Dostoyevsky of his time. No—better yet—he was the Raskolnikov of his time. He caroused all around Paris and wrote mocking wills and bawdy verses."

"Bawdy? What kind of word is bawdy?"

"It's a good word. Probably of Anglo–Saxon origin."

"Mom! How many times must I tell you, I do not want to know any word's origin," Cosmo said. "It's a ridiculous word. It's the kind of word Jean-Claude would have used."

"He might have, if he spoke English," I said. "Which is doubtful. More likely Latin was his second language. But let's just leave Villon out of it, then. Just remember Joan of Arc's deplorable martyrdom. You have no excuse for not knowing when she died."

"I don't need an excuse," Cosmo said.

I didn't agree. It seemed to me that there could never have been a time when either of my children did not know of the lamentable conflagration of Joan of Arc, the Maid of Orleans, the Savior of France. And when it occurred.

Cosmo said, "I can't believe you didn't remember the number I gave you. All you had to do was remember four little numbers."

I said, "Well, now you can remember four little numbers, numbers with meaning."

Cosmo swatted the top of his head in mock dismay, and appeared to be completely mesmerized by the darkening horizon.

The Knife

I t was still the early-morning myopia-induced fuzz. I heard Gus ask rhetorically: "Who made the bloody mess with all the bloody towels?" Of course he knew. If Gus had not made the bloody mess himself, then I was the only possible suspect. Cosmo was still sleeping, and would be for hours. I was wending my way down the back stairs toward the kitchen, from whence one often heard ejaculations and eruptions not necessarily intended for one's ears. The back stairs were an obstacle course composed of stacks of books on subjects of current interest, such as Nicaraguan shark hunters, or sixteenth-century English martyrs, or youth hostels in Europe, or PCB's in the Hudson, or French Symbolist poetry, or Russian novels of ennui. These interests were in constant flux, and therefore the stacks and the obstacle course were subject to unannounced changes.

"Whom do you think?" I said, as precisely as possible, which was not very, because in fact the loss of blood coupled with the sight of blood unnerved me.

"What happened?"

"I was attacked again by the knife you left in the sink.

Pretty soon I'll be down to counting by nines and eights,"
I said.

"Ah, base-eight," said Gus, who knew far more of math
than I did, and liked to remind me of the fact.

"Have you seen my glasses this morning?" I asked. Often
in the night my eyeglasses hid themselves under my pillow
or under my bed, and in the mornings I would wander in a
daze until I located a second pair that would enable me to
find the first, the lost, the prodigal pair of glasses. Without
which the world was impressionistically beautiful and
devoid of its cutting edges.

"They're where you left them," Gus said.

I opened the freezer and extracted two ice cubes. I applied
one to my newly sliced left ring finger, and one I rubbed on
my temples. It was over eighty degrees Fahrenheit in April in
New York, at eight in the morning. This was not normal.

I have always thought weather was interesting, unseasonable extremes of weather being extremely interesting.
When it was tropical in New York in April, I wanted to share
the news with all my correspondents, especially those not
quite so blessed with unnatural weather phenomena.

In response to my weather and injury update, my friend
Rachel in California sent me this e-mail:

> *There are several reasons why it is so hot. One has to do with the knife
> in the sink. The others will be revealed. None of them good.*

During that spring I had too often cut myself with the big
kitchen knife. Uncorrected myopia or strabismus played a
part in these mishaps, but they were not the only causation.

The scenario was always the same: the very sharpest of our kitchen knives would be lying in the bottom of the sink and in my panic to clean the dishes and erase evidence of all those eaten meals, I would grab hold of the blade or the blade would leap up at me, or I would simply be reaching for the charred potato pot and en route the knife's blade would delve to within millimeters of my finger bone, on occasion even severing the *flexores digitorum.* Some people would learn not to stick their fingers into places where dangerous objects might lie. Others might learn to never enter the kitchen without their favorite pair of horn-rim glasses.

These wounds bled profusely. After bleeding profusely, they took an excessively long time to heal, presumably because my fingers could not be inactive and so the wounds were never left untouched to heal themselves. Band-Aids lived up to the use for which they have become a universal metaphor: a temporary and essentially useless stopgap measure. I experimented with different types of Band-Aids: with Clear ones that were almost invisible (their intention being to not call attention to the wound in question, which was not always my intention); with Flexible fabric ones, which stayed on better than most until they became wet and then they were heavy and soggy like paper diapers in a swimming pool; with Sports ones, which stayed on best of all but did not allow the wound to breathe; with Fingertip and Knuckle ones, so beautifully specific to my digital cuts; and finally with neon pink Band-Aids and leopard-skin Band-Aids and zebra-stripe Band-Aids. Those last were my favorites.

It is a fact that it is awkward to type when one has injured fingers. When swathed in a Band-Aid the fingertips are larger than normal and therefore cumbersome. Without Band-Aids, the sliced finger pads are raw and exposed and liable at any moment to bleed anew.

Almost every day I exchanged with Rachel in California e-mails on a variety of subjects including but not limited to her lifelong feud with her father about her mother's money, and her Nordic stepmother, and her love affairs with the Hispanic boxers in Los Angeles, and the buses she rode in Los Angeles and the fame she thereby acquired as the only white person riding buses in Los Angeles, and the carpenter bees under my front porch and my fruitless efforts to persuade them to gnaw on rotten wood elsewhere, and the ocular diseases to which my beloved bulldog was subject, and the lives of the saints, mostly female saints who suffered terribly, like Lydwin of Schiedam and Mariana of Quito who slept in her coffin every Friday night. And since the finger cuts affected my typing and were making me prone to typos and Freudian slips, I also wrote to Rachel about the knives in the sink and the bleeding fingers that were hampering my normally excellent typing.

Rachel quickly determined that there was nothing accidental about the cuts, or the knife. She wrote:

Ok, now regarding that knife in the sink which you sliced your fuck-you finger on. Of course Gus left it there on purpose, hoping you would land it in your heart. Whatever, you must write about this. Perhaps a good story would be called Household Chores.

I could not imagine a worse title than Household Chores.

But Rachel has never shied away from telling me what she thinks, and what I should do with my life, and what is ridiculous about my life. I first met her almost thirty years ago. We were both attending a writers' conference in Iowa, a state I had hitherto only associated with highways that allowed for unimpeded speeding. Some trick of fate had arranged for us to share a small dorm room, and that very first night, as I was undressing and about to slip my Lanz flannel nightgown over my head, Rachel said, "Did you have polio when you were a child?"

I had in fact not had polio as a child, or ever. I did have very thin legs at the time, but not sickly thin, not in my opinion. Rachel was shorter and heftier than me. She considered my flannel nightgowns and espadrilles to be emblematic of some arcane New England life that I assured her I did not lead. That made no difference to her.

Since then I have apparently been a source of constant humor to Rachel. After the espadrilles she found my clogs to be equally ridiculous. She considered my maternal paeans to the beauty and brains of my children to be painfully evocative of Greek tragedy. One of the things I loved about Rachel was her willingness to exaggerate and indulge in melodrama. It seemed to me that while I probably had the same impulses, my superego was intact.

After the third cut, this time on my right thumb, Rachel wrote me:

> *As for the knife: I suppose what is significant is not whether it was put there deliberately, by whatever forces, but that you did not "anticipate"*

*its lying in wait for you. AND that your finger hurts as a reminder of
all those wounds that were inflicted upon you, self-inflicted upon you,
as a way of——?*

*Wounds serve a purpose beyond the obvious, beyond the "pain" and
it is ESSENTIAL that at some point you examine this, through your
writing, not through your conscious.*

*As in: He left it here, he wanted to kill me, maim me, awake me,
nurse me, whatever. The literal, the obvious never applies in these
matters.*

*But you have enough experience with knives and other vessels that
cause you pain to have at least begun to develop some intuitive knowledge about where they are to avoid them. Or not.*

I e-mailed back to Rachel and reminded her that I had
spent several years in therapy and was no longer kept awake
at night by fond memories of an anguished childhood I had
probably never had. What did she mean by my experience
with knives?

The knife in question, the one that kept slicing through
my flesh, had long ago been a wedding gift from a man we
had known in college in California. He had been a neighbor
of Gus's pot connection, which was how we'd originally
gotten to know him. He and the pot connection followed
what I now think of as an essentially Californian trajectory:
in college they smoked pot and were vaguely liberal, after
college they became entrepreneurs or politicians. The knife
donor went on to Washington and worked in the office of a
California congressman who years later went down, in a
blaze of unglory, in a scandal involving water rights and
immigrant children. I knew that Skip, our friend, had a

crush on me and that because he was overweight he was very shy and would never say anything indecorous, especially as Gus and I had been together since what appeared to have been my infancy. Once, when I visited other friends in Washington, I let him take me out to dinner, and I was—I see this now—cruelly oblivious to his affections. Then Gus and I got married and Skip sent us a large steel kitchen knife. Of course there was a penny taped to the inside lid of the box. Little did I know. When it came, and as I was opening wedding gifts and making lists for the voluble thank-you notes I would later write, I showed the penny to my mother.

"It's for luck," she said.

"Good or bad?" I asked.

"Good, I should imagine," she said. All the wedding business and brouhaha, and my unchic desire to let her make all the decisions, was wearing Mother down. She had her own life awaiting her, but I could only see all our lives as revolving around this epochal event—my nuptial vows—after which I would no longer doubt my choices and life would make sense and children would sprout in the interstices between the cherry tomatoes and the dahlias.

"It's bad luck to give a knife without a coin. Because they sever love. And friendship also," Mom said.

"Then why take the risk and give a knife at all?" I said. "I mean, we could buy our own knives."

"But a good knife is extremely useful. Really a cook's most precious implement. This seems like a good one—it's real steel so you can sharpen it ad infinitum."

"Will I want to?"

"Sharpen it? If you want to cut anything other than butter."

I am sure I wrote a charming thank-you note. Writing elaborate and smarmy thank-you notes was one of my talents, if you could call it that. I didn't understand then what my mother meant about real steel; now I do. It was not stainless. The knife was quickly and permanently stained a mottled black, and it could be honed again and again. As a child, I'd watched my father spit on his whetstone and then rub the knife's blade in quick circular motions. Sparks flew. I could have sworn that sparks flew. So when I had my own knife and my own whetstone, and spit my own spit, I tried to imitate his motions. But because they were hesitant, they were also slower than my father's, and no sparks flew. Not from that particular whetstone. Which one was defective: the knife, the stone, the spit, or the whetter?

I'm much speedier these days with the blade and the stone, but still.

This is the knife that has cut into all my finger pads more than once, that has severed digital nerves, and once grazed the distal phalanx of my Fuck-you finger.

I sent Rachel an e-mail telling her about Skip and the knife and the penny. She wrote back:

Like a dormant virus, it's been there all along and your continued ignorance, idiocy, blindness is getting beyond my powers for commentary and critique and analysis.

No, that will never happen.

Get rid of the knife, and get a grip.

Of course I had no intention of getting rid of the knife. It was far and away my best kitchen knife. With it, I'd cut through the rib cage of scores of chicken and hens, I'd shaved off dark chocolate, I'd cored and diced Granny Smith's and Northern Spies, I'd sliced Yukon Golds for perfect frites. A culinary Sherlock Holmes could have reconstructed the history of our diets from this one knife. It would be a gold-mine for archeologists of the future. It went nowhere I did not go. And vice versa, I think.

But the bloody fingertips were becoming a hindrance in so many ways. Spring was also the time of year of oniongrass, when I ruthlessly yanked those feculent tubers from my flower beds, and thus the time of year when my fingers smelled of oniongrass, which is not the same as smelling of onions. Theirs is a pungent, skanky smell of the compost heap rather than the abattoir.

My ability to weed with a vengeance—the only way to weed—was impaired by the sliced fingers. It also transpired that the odors of oniongrass lodged themselves in the cuts with a tenacity unobtainable on unsliced skin, wherever that might lie. Whenever I weeded out the oniongrass, I thought of durian, an Asian fruit I have never seen, never tasted, never smelled. But everyone I have ever known who has returned from southeast Asia has felt compelled to describe the experience of eating durian, and thus it has gained a sticky foothold in my psyche.

Durian is "spherical fruit, six to eight inches in diameter. It has a hard external husk, or shell, covered with coarse spines, and contains five oval compartments, each filled with cream-colored, custardlike pulp, in which are embedded from one to five chestnut-sized seeds. The pulp is edible and the seeds may be eaten if roasted." My friends all swore it was delicious, but it is not exported. Too bad for the rest of you. The encyclopedia describes durian's odor as of "rotten onions or sewage." The OED says it has a "strong civet odor." That was all very well and good. I didn't expect olfactory verisimilitude from the dictionary. But every one of my peripatetic friends said that durian smelled just like a woman having sex, specifically, like a woman's sex. Or like dead fish, there being apparently a strong similarity.

That was what I thought of whenever I smelled my fingers after pulling up oniongrass weeds, which was all the time in the spring. And with my fingers smelling so skanky, I needed to remember not to visit the manicurist or go to the jeweler's to try on diamond rings, in case they might wonder where those fingers had been, assuming they had imaginations like mine, like sewers.

So, later in the day, I asked Gus to please stop leaving the knife in the sink, blade up and poised for the kill. (There was never any danger of Gus himself actually delving into the kitchen sink, that snakepit, that midden of offal. Gus sometimes cooked but never cleaned up because the soap bubbles might destroy his sensitive olfactory organs, which were so essential to his culinary creativity. How else could he have conceived of stuffing an enchilada with parsnips and parsley? The literary merits of alliteration do not necessarily translate into successful recipes, I told him. *Viz.* macaroni and mackerel. He was not amused.)

"Maybe you should look before you stick your hands in the sink," he said.

"That's not the point," I said. "Of course I look. It's just that I can't always see. And I shouldn't have to always be anticipating a land mine. As it were."

"Spare me."

"I'm not kidding," I said. "Look at these bloody fingers. How would you like to spend forty-five minutes in the Band-Aid aisle?"

"No comment."

"Oh, I suppose you look carefully every time you place your foot on the floor. Of course not, you just assume that there will be no broken glass."

"But I would look first if I were to put my foot in the sink," Gus said.

"Rachel thinks you leave the knife there on purpose," I said.

"And what purpose does she have in mind?"

"To kill me. To stab me through the heart."

Like a sailboat changing tack, Gus's whole body shifted when I said that. "And you believe her? That woman is a certified lunatic," he said.

"Isn't that like the kettle calling the pot burned?" I said.

That evening, after dining on a smorgasbord of flatulence-inducing legumes, I almost severed the distal portion of my left ring finger. But it was the shock that made me cry, not the pain. What was surprising about it? Surely not that I had cut myself again. No, it had something to do with seeing the danger of relaxed vigilance, and the psychological implications thereof. I painfully typed an e-mail and sent it to Rachel, who volleyed back through cyberspace:

You know your pattern re injuries. You seem to have a "need" to keep reopening "old" wounds so to speak . . . perhaps it is a way of grounding yourself and keeping things in "order." WHO AM I to say that there are other ways. Whatever works.

I wrote back that it was either a pattern or a plot, but I denied that it would be both. And why all the quotation marks?

It was later, in brilliant June, when my brother James and his wife, Inga, and their five blond, myopic children came to visit. They came through once each year on their northerly trek to Maine. They always arrived in two enormous vehicles, a Decimator and a Humungouster. Inga drove the larger of the two, and the two girls rode with her. James drove the smaller, with the three boys. Each vehicle theoretically had seating for nine persons. I loved watching their caravan pull into the driveway, in tandem, meticulously packed like Chinese puzzle boxes, surmounted by kayaks and umiaks and canoes and Zodiaks, piggybacked with numerous bicycles. After eight-plus hours of driving from a state below the Mason–Dixon line, they always, year after year, arrived within one or two minutes of the appointed time. Were it not for the unfortunate pointy chin we share,

I would be hard put to believe the genetic link between James and me.

But this arrival was different from all his other arrivals, because for the first time they came accompanied by messy and hungry and noisy baby robins. A nestful of robins. Just before leaving, explained Katerina (age seven, the fourth), they had seen the mother robin keel over and die, leaving behind these orphans. Bartholomew (at fourteen the oldest boy, generally assumed to have been switched at birth, on account of his predilection for stand-up comedy, however bad) gave an unconvincing but very amusing rendition of the mother robin developing angina, clutching herself with her wings, losing her balance, teetering precariously, bemoaning the impending orphanhood of her chicks, and finally toppling from her perch. So then, having already watched as the speckled eggs were laid and cosseted and hatched, the children deemed it impossible (not to mention inhumane) to leave the robins motherless and hungry. Neither James nor Inga cared much for animals; they considered my doting fondness for Saint Joan to be a sign of mental derangement. Given Saint Joan's remarkable looks—she was a slightly lame bulldog bitch with congenital entropion and random bald patches whenever her seasonal alopecia got out of hand— many people said similar things in jest, but James said it completely seriously. James said almost nothing in jest. But to give him credit, he had spawned children with tenderer feelings than his for the animal kingdom, and they refused to go off to a pristine northern lake while the robins starved.

The robins were, in fact, again approaching starvation.

Their southern worm supply had been exhausted somewhere on the New Jersey Turnpike, and the chicks were
puling with hunger. The first thing we did upon their arrival
was head out back to the compost heap with a couple of
trowels, and start digging for worms. There were lots of
worms, but somehow not quite as many worms as I'd initially imagined. And significant digging was required, and
worms did not necessarily make themselves available for
plucking. Rather, it seemed that whenever a trowel or an
eager finger got near, the worms wriggled their way deeper
into the brown, moist breeding medium, the earth. And
then, even when I made contact with or actually gained
purchase on the head or tail of a worm, often the prey
would slither away or break in half, leaving me with less
food. Had I given it any thought, I would have put on gloves
prior to this foraging—although they would no doubt have
clumsified my worm-grabbers. As it was, the cuts and gashes
and gouges on my pinky and my raw Fuck-you finger and
my index finger were soon filled with dirt, and throbbing.
They smelled, as always, of oniongrass, and of something
else, not quite shit, but close.

The fat nightcrawlers were the easiest to grab hold of, but
we all agreed that they were seriously gross, obese, and
glutted with blood (whose we did not ask). They were so
large that if fed directly into the open mouths of the robins,
the chicks might choke. So we had to chop up the nightcrawlers. This task was, to my dismay, assigned to me.

I sang along with Katerina and Conrad (five years old and
the youngest), the two most devoted worm-diggers:

Nobody loves me
Everybody hates me
I'm going to go eat worms.
Big fat juicy ones
Long lean skinny ones,
Gosh, how the little ones squirm.
Bite the heads off, Suck the juice out,
Throw the skins away.
You'd be surprised how man can survive
On worms three times a day.

Katerina was pale, miniature, and elfin, all of which traits belied her repertoire of grotesque doggerel and her delight in creatures more often regarded with disdain, if not horror: the creepy-crawlies, the toads, the slugs, the arthropods. Her more squeamish elder siblings were by no means so catholic in their zoological pursuits. And for Katerina, the payoff was happening that evening, as she was clearly the chief feeder of the chicks, dangling and then dropping the worms into the wide-open infant beaks. They appeared to have a seamless, bend-free duct going directly from gaping maw to anus, so quickly did the limey bird poop follow upon the worm ingestion.

We were sitting on the terrace digesting our dinner, watching the fireflies in the field blink their messages to the heavens, to the aliens, to each other. Katerina and Conrad and Ralph were still busy with the baby robins; their hunger was endless.

James said, "Do you notice anything weird about me?"

"More than usual?" Cosmo said.

"No, seriously, do you notice anything different?"

I looked carefully. Less hair? No. Had he gained weight? Not so I would notice. Had he pierced an earlobe? No. "I give up," I said. "Am I terribly unobservant?"

"Probably not," Inga said.

"Absolutely," Cosmo said.

James went on, "I just wanted to warn you first. I've developed a tic."

"A tic tic, or a Rocky Mountain Spotted Fever tick, or a dreaded Lyme disease tick?"

"A tic tic," he said.

Inga said, "It's called a tic douloureux, or Trigeminal neuralgia."

"How did you do that?" I said. "I don't see it."

"It's like this," he said and then he deliberately sent his upper right cheek muscle twitching in the direction of his temple. This was obviously something only an accomplished actor could produce on demand, so James deserved a certain credit. But I was struck by something else, an eerie and completely vivid childhood memory.

"Wow. Just like Tante Odile," I blurted.

"Exactly," said Cosmo, which surprised me because I could never tell how closely he observed the older and more foreign members of the family.

"I'd rather you didn't say that," James said. Tante Odile was our now aged French maiden aunt. Actually, she was not really an aunt but something more like a second stepcousin twice removed, some relationship better understood in France and better expressed in French. She was extremely cantankerous, bigoted, and hypochondriac. No one would want to be compared to her. But she did have a remarkable facial tic: a Napoleon of facial tics, a Quasimodo of facial tics, a Rasputin of facial tics. In our distant childhoods, we had spent hours watching her tic, trying to predict its next appearance, and practicing our imitations.

"I get your point," I said. "But it was one hell of a déjà vu, or maybe more like a beaucoup déjà vu."

Gus said, "Your Tante Odile never once remembered my name, not after twenty-odd years of being married to Ursula." He always said this about Tante Odile. It was becoming clear to me, after the aforementioned twenty years, that he actually minded.

"Don't feel too special," James said.

"She forgets everyone's name, whether she likes them or not," I said.

Cosmo said, "It must be a French thing. Like their inability to tell jokes."

"How would you know they don't tell jokes when you don't speak a word of French?" I asked.

"I just know these things," Cosmo said, with that infuriating smugness of the specious arguer who knows that he has already led you merrily past any hope for logical discussion.

"The best mimes are all French," I pointed out.

"And what is it that mimes do not do? Tell jokes. Point taken," said Cosmo.

Inga turned to me and asked, "What is Cosmo's problem

with the French? I was unaware he had a prejudiced bone in his body."

"Only against dorks," I said. "The French thing is a genetic defect, from his father's side of course. It's totally illogical— they all love French wine, but seem to find nothing funnier than to do their Three Stooges routines with French accents."

"Is *that* what you thought has been going on?" Gus asked, with mild indignation. "Do you mean to say that our brilliant send-ups of Gallic foibles has been wasted on you?"

"Ha ha," I said. "So let's get back to the tic."

"I've been to a neurologist," James said.

"And she said?"

"He's still doing tests," James said.

"You do know that most tics are NOT St. Vitus's dance or epilepsy, and are psychological in origin?" I said. "So, do you have a long-suppressed desire to be a French virgin? Or is it just your bestial impulses struggling to break out?"

James said "You're not funny."

Bartholomew, with Katerina astride his shoulders, having just completed yet another course in the Meal of Worms, said, "Actually, Dad, it is kind of funny."

"But is it painful?"

"Is what painful?" James said.

"The tic. What else?"

"Not especially. Not that it's comfortable, mind you."

Bartholomew said, "I read in the encyclopedia that tics occur with decreasing frequency from head to foot."

"They're not the only things," Gus said.

"Well, I've been giving this some thought," Bartholomew went on. "What else falls into that category? Hair? Ideas?"

"Hats," said Katerina.

"Pimples," suggested Cosmo. He was seventeen and therefore acquainted with this dermatological phenomenon, but I had never heard him actually pronounce the word. Unlike Anglo—Saxon expletives, it had been implicitly taboo in our home.

"Hey, that's good," Bartholomew said. "It's sort of in the same class of annoyance."

"I hardly think a zit is as annoying as a tic," James said.

"You know what I mean, Dad."

Then Cosmo got up and started clearing away plates, and the other children followed him. They did not return to the table; they continued on into some distant part of the house where, I suspected, he was sharing with them something their parents would not approve of, and for which they would later lament the pernicious influence of my darling Cosmo. Something like his stash of fireworks or his collection of rap CDs with highly offensive language. I'd heard the CDs and I knew of the existence of the fireworks, although I'd never managed to find them.

It happened again while I was washing up after dinner. This time it was the proximal phalanx of my right baby finger that was almost severed. I was shocked. I had thought that I had braced myself, taken precautions. I felt like a young woman for whom no amount of birth control is ever enough to counteract her luminous and earthy fertility. She would always get pregnant, and my fingers would always gravitate towards the sharpened blade of the stained and notched wedding present. Maybe there were infinitesimal bits of magnetic substance in my fingers that drew them inexorably towards the blade. But I didn't believe that at all. At least a cut on my pinkie would not affect my typing skills, because I'd never managed to put my pinkie to any use on the keyboard. But even so, it bled and bled and made me weep for self-pity, after which I chastised myself for the self-piteous whimpering. My mother had not fallen off a branch and died and left me hungry. My facial muscles were not involuntarily contracting. What had I to complain of?

I do not think you can accurately remember acquiring many of your injuries, you simply ascribe circumstances and situations which seem to explain how they appeared but in truth they are old wounds which you seem to feel the need to reopen, as I have said. I suspect it has to do with your birthday, your relationship with your children, your father, and god knows where the planets are. I HOPE you will not find it necessary to do permanent damage in order to achieve some sort of release or relief or whatever it is these wounds seek to remind you of. PAIN.

That night there was a raucous, operatic, bombastic thunderstorm, like something out of Verdi's *Nabucco* or Wagner's *Siegfried*. While Gus slept on, I found myself upright on my side of the bed. Saint Joan pushed open the bedroom door with her flat nose that quivered in terror. Her entire round body shook without cease. For a while I lay next to her on the floor and held her tight, as if by pressure I could keep her heart from bursting through her rib cage and exploding in the room. But neither the thunderclaps nor the searing strikes of lightning abated, and Saint Joan's quaking exhausted both of us, so I lifted her onto my bed—she was unable to climb up herself. All night long, the mattress vibrated like one of those No-Tell Motel beds: five minutes for a quarter.

In the morning Katerina said that she'd been awakened by the storm and that she'd pulled the covers over her head and read *Runaway Bunny* by flashlight, over and over again. James's children were never without flashlights or books, one of their most endearing traits. It turned out that everyone else had slept soundly and dreamed of the birds.

Then we went back to the compost heap to collect more worms for the final leg of their journey to Maine.

After they left, I returned to the kitchen and located the knife. I taped a penny to the blade, and then wrapped it in several layers of the *New York Times* Style Section and then sealed it up with masking tape. Having thus protected our trash collectors or any random scavengers from injuring themselves in ways I was all too familiar with, I put the knife in the garbage.

All day long I felt eerily chipper. I was efficient. I was light-hearted. I wrote letters that had been demanding responses for weeks. I reorganized the linen closet. I found all the books about birds from all the different rooms in the house and piled them on the bench in the kitchen. I finished *Oblomov* and Rousseau's *Confessions,* two of the many unfinished books in a stack next to my bed. Then I went to the garden to dig and plant and tamp down earth. I yanked up onion-grass with impunity.

It was dusk when I returned to the kitchen to wash my hands. There in the sink, like a snake in the grass, like a scorpion in the sand, was the knife, just lying there in the bottom of the sink, as if that were the most normal thing in the world.

"What is the knife doing there?" I bellowed.

Nothing. No thunder, no lightning, no Saint Joan vibrating like a sausage on a conveyor belt, and certainly no Gus.

"This knife is not supposed to be here," I said. And then Gus materialized, so suddenly it was as if he'd been napping inside the refrigerator.

"I'd like to know what that murderous knife is doing in the sink," I said.

"Absolutely nothing," said Gus. When I became most upset, he would become most literal. It was an unfortunate pattern we had developed over those many years of marital volleyball.

"Stop it. How did it get there?"

"I put it there."

"You put it there? It was in the trash. It was wrapped up better than a dead body. Why did you take it out of the trash when clearly someone meant it to be there?"

"Because it's the best knife. I need it," Gus said.

"I hate that knife," I said. "I used to think it was a good knife, but I have changed my mind. That knife is a deadly weapon. It's taken on some evil personality all its own, like some teenage horror movie. I now regard that knife as the

Quisling, the Malinche, the Judas Iscariot, the Benedict Arnold, the Kim Philby of knives."

"But it's the only decently sharp knife we have."

I started sniffling. "Are you listening? I can't live in the same house with that knife anymore. That knife has turned against me—me, who has kept it and used it and washed it probably thousands of times. I regard that as betrayal, or worse."

"What is worse than that?"

"Forget it," I said. "It was just an expression. Forget the bloody knife."

The chicks were DOA in Maine. Bartholomew called with the news. I could hear Katerina's weeping in the background.

"Let me talk to your dad," I said.

James came on the line. "I knew those birds were a mistake," he said.

"Jamesie," I said. "I didn't mean to make light of your tic. I just didn't want you to get too upset, or too attached."

"It's hard not to be attached to one's face," he said.

"And it's a very nice face."

Later I sent Rachel an e-mail about the knife that was resurrected from the garbage, and the dead orphan birds.

She wrote, *Why don't you stop telling me the same stories and go see a psychic. Bring the knife with you. Or bury it in the backyard.*

I explained that burying the knife was out of the question. I could not live and imagine how, in some future garden, there would be an unsuspecting planter and weeder who would reach into the earth for a tasty worm, and come up with a bloody semisevered finger.

Forget burying, she countered. *Since the knife is clearly not going anywhere, perhaps you should.*

Then a small package arrived from Maine, a package that appeared to come from another era. It was a shoebox tenderly wrapped in brown paper and tied with twine. The addresses, to and from, bore the careful flourishes and serifs of the newfound script of Katerina Auxerre. Inside were five tiny baby robin corpses, and a note in that same script: *We think they should be burried in your gardden.*

What else could I do? I wound heavy-duty electrical tape round and round the blade of the knife, and put it inside the shoebox. I buried the box, with the note and the knife, in a corner of the yard where I liked to think no one would be digging or gardening. And I made a little cairn atop the site.

That evening Gus wanted to grill some eggplants and parsnips, and was looking for the knife in order to thinly slice them.

"Okay, I give up," he said. "Where is it this time?"

"This time it has been given a fitting burial. Along with the chicks—remember?—from Katerina."

"You're kidding."

"I would hardly kid about this," I said.

"You're right," he said. "Your sense of humor seems to abandon you in the face of that bloody knife."

"Not bloody anymore," I said.

"Actually," Gus said, "this is kind of like burying the hatchet."

"Oh," I said. "That's funny."

"Are we referring to funny-haha or funny-peculiar or funny-rowboat?" he said.

"Yes," I said. Because this was suddenly the best and kindest thing he could have said. It was something his cousin Malone always said. When Malone first made the quip it was simply odd. There really is an obsolete definition of funny as a rowboat, actually a "narrow, clinker-built pleasure-boat for a pair of sculls. Also loosely, any light boat." Around the tenth time Malone said it, it was simply peculiar and idiosyn-cratic. But the hundredth time it was truly funny, weepingly funny, and emblematic of his humorous and tenuous grip on life. I loved Malone, who was slowly dying, and loving him was something Gus and I had always done well together.

The Phantom Limb

When I first heard about the dominatrix in the state of Maine, I was driving west and it was raining in that forlorn stretch of Connecticut where it is always raining.

On past trips Winnie and Cosmo, my children, had postulated that Connecticut was like Jupiter, where they say a huge anticyclone or vortex has been raging for centuries and will continue raging, and which accounts for The Great Red Spot that blankets the planet. We wondered about conditions underneath that spot. Was a storm on Jupiter like a monsoon, or more like El Niño, or like a Grade Five Hurricane named Gabriella? All we knew was that on Jupiter the clouds were made of frozen ammonia crystals. My children liked to point that out, but I never knew why.

I only know that Connecticut always came between us in New York and grandparents in Maine; and in Connecticut it was risky to speed, on account of the unpleasantly vigilant state troopers, and it always rained whenever I drove through, the kind of rain that dented the roof of the car and poured down the windshield like a cataract. *Gullywashers* was the meteorological term for this rain.

But this time, driving alone, I cranked up the volume to hear the news on Public Radio. In conjunction with its planetary weather patterns, Connecticut was also a radio wasteland, from which only NPR occasionally emerged like some skeletal survivor arriving at an oasis. Winnie once told me that Jupiter was a source of radio transmissions. Not exactly radio transmissions, not a Prairie Jove Companion exactly, but the planet was a source of two types of emissions, decameter radiation, the erratic bursts, and decimeter radiation, the continuous source.

But that time hearing about the dominatrix, I was driving alone and so there was no one to complain about the volume or the static. Only Hildegard von Bingen, and I fed her biscuits at regular intervals and she snored in the backseat on her drool-encrusted blanket. Hildy was our new bulldog, still almost a puppy. There had been months of discussion about whether or not to get another bulldog after Saint Joan's lingering death, her blindness and emphysema and deep depression. But there had never been any real doubt. And although it had taken several forms of emotional blackmail to persuade my family to allow me to name her for Hildegard, they were now as devoted to and besotted with Hildy as could be desired.

The rain and the static and the snoring are the auditory setting I must draw around what comes next, a preemptive strike against doubt, skepticism, my own or yours.

On the NPR news I heard a piece about a man, a dead man now, who had been dismembered by a dominatrix in Bangor, Maine. The gist of the piece seemed to be that the man, the client, Mr. Milquetoast as I thought of him, had been killed or even just died by accident in the course of being dominated by Madame Thong, as I thought of her. There were no details. Or were there? I continued through the driving rain and imagined games that involved near-misses with poleaxes (the two-headed kind favored by Barbarians, and Goths and Vandals), and whippings that got out of hand as a Sufi-esque frenzy took over their pleasures. Somehow at the end poor Mr. Milquetoast was dead, and Madame Thong had a dead body to dispose of. And faced with the reality of that dead body and the undesirability of calling her local funeral parlor, she determined to use the tools at hand and dismember poor Mr. Milquetoast and then dispose separately of the individual parts.

None of these finer points was on NPR. I was busy working out the minutiae of my scenario and so I did not catch any perky station-identification spots. Instead, it occurred to me that to dismember a body is harder than it sounds. Certainly I've separated many chicken wings from their adjacent breasts, and truncated the ribs of lamb crown roasts; but when you consider severing a human arm from its trunk, you can see that you would need a serious knife and there would be the problem of blood drainage, and other problems that I am sure I cannot even imagine.

And what about his clothes? What did Madame Thong do with Mr. Milquetoast's flannel-lined jeans and plaid shirt and L.L. Bean Gore-Tex and Thinsulate hunting boots, the ones with lace-up leather tops and rubber soles? Did her clothes come from L.L. Bean as well? What in the catalog could be creatively altered to suit a dominatrix fantasy? I always thought the Baxter State parka with a fur-lined hood had great potential. Or am I so parochial, so pathetically urban as to not realize that black thongs and leather bodices and lace-up boots and whips and chains are as available in Bangor, Maine as anywhere else, if you know where to look?

Back when Winnie and Cosmo were young, back before they got driver's licenses and lives of their own, back when their only way from New York to their grandparents in Maine was in the same car with their mother or father or both, they expended much of their apparently infinite supply of energy on the problem of the eradication or shrinking of the state of Connecticut.

Winnie favored a direct meteor hit that would carve out a crater so deep that the edges of Connecticut would cave in enough that the actual perimeter of the state would be reduced to about five miles. Then we could cross the crater on a vast suspension bridge, and stare into the abyss. Cosmo's plan, not surprisingly, was even more explosive, more inflammatory. He liked to describe a perfectly contained detonation that would reduce the state to a small pile of ash, something unnoticed by the side of the road. He had always enjoyed watching my brother Gabriel's collection of home videos of buildings being razed with the wrecking ball, or selectively imploded. My suggestion was a small cross at the rest area off 684, where better-hearted souls could lay floral wreaths at the remains of Connecticut. Both Winnie and Cosmo considered that weak-minded of me.

I arrived back in New York just in time to say good-bye to

Gus as he went off for a week at tennis camp. He claimed he had told me he was going, but I had no recollection. Absolutely none. I was sure if he had told me I would have remembered because I would have been so grateful that I was not going off to tennis camp: eight hours a day of batting blindly at a small green ball that was never quite where I thought it should be. The whole thing sounded like a terrible idea to me, an unfortunate return to my benighted days at St. Elmo's Girls Academy, and my constant struggle to invent new excuses for not attending gym class. It was only after Gus and all his extra tennis rackets had left for their camp, that I began to wonder about that NPR report on the dominatrix in Maine. I began to doubt whether I had heard what I thought I heard, or whether I had heard it all.

There seemed to be no other evidence of this salacious item. I read all of the *Times* and the *Boston Globe* without encountering a shred of a dominatrix in Maine, and no dismemberments of any kind. Then I went online to the Portland and Bangor newspapers and entered as keywords both *dominatrix* and *dismember,* to no avail. I entered them separately and then in combination. You can imagine the results.

Finally I called my younger sister who actually lives in the state of Maine. It is true that Sophie is more likely to know of threats to the Northern Forest or the population count of plankton in Casco Bay than about a dominatrix in Bangor, but I thought that surely such a bizarre story might have caught her eye or ear, even if it was only while en route to witness a dam removal on the Kennebec River.

But no.

She and her husband both said they would look around for it in local articles or on the Web, but I never heard from them, and I doubted they tried very hard, if at all.

Meanwhile, for the second time that summer, and on the very day that Gus left, the kitchen sink backed up without any warning. The strange thing was that since he'd stopped working in the city he rarely left the house at all anymore. And when he did, the occasions proved momentous, or symptomatic. First he went to Amsterdam, for reasons I preferred not to know. Then he went to tennis camp. Both times the kitchen sink filled almost to the brim with slimy grayish water in which floated all sorts of bits and pieces of meals eaten and uneaten.

It didn't back up the third time he went away and it was a lucky thing, because that was when I went into the hospital to have the cyst removed from my wrist. But we'll get back to that.

It was clogging for the second time when I pondered ways of learning more about the dominatrix. I called several numbers for National Public Radio, and they had no idea what I was talking about. I said that I had heard it while in Connecticut, if that would help. It didn't.

First I vigorously plunged with the so-called plumber's friend, which was no friend of mine, perhaps because I was not a plumber. Was I using it under false pretenses? Then I outfitted myself with a surgical mask and latex gloves—because I was instructed to do so—and poured into the kitchen sink a toxic substance guaranteed to break through any clog, any blockage caused by any amount of regurgitated food, detritus, grease, hair, and other unmentionables. But nothing I did or could do, so it seemed, made the least difference to the stagnant pool in the kitchen sink. I gave up and called the plumber.

There it was: the sink was still full of tepid fetid water and small parts of food waste that were rapidly becoming unidentifiable except perhaps to a gastronomic pathologist. I have been reticent to call in the plumber ever since a series of incidents with the downstairs toilet that occurred when Cosmo was three or four.

Those many years ago, I was already fairly adept at plunging (back when I thought we were friends) or even snaking out minor plumbing backups. So when Winnie announced that the bowl was overflowing and water was cascading onto the bathroom floor, I went in with a beach towel and a plunger. I plunged and I plunged, but I was unsuccessful. I mopped up the floor and got the toilet to stop flooding, but I couldn't get it to flush without a recurrence. So I called the plumbers.

In those days, I was already acquainted with the Pentimenti brothers, Rocco and Dominic. One was tall and handsome, the other was tall and not handsome. They were both laconic in the extreme, a situation that compelled me to make idiotic conversation. The handsome one, Rocco, also had a port wine stain on his left cheek, which of course I could not stop looking at. Rocco came that afternoon, or rather dusk. I remember the falling light. It did not take him long to solve the problem. He emerged from the bathroom with a pink plastic leg.

"Do you recognize this?" he asked me.

It was about nine inches long and not remotely anatomi-
cally correct. Winnie sauntered by, saw it, and wailed,
"Barbie!"

"Not Barbie," I said, suddenly realizing whose leg it was.
"Look, the foot is flat. No high heels. Barbie always wears
high heels."

"Ken," she wailed again, and went off in search of her
brother. Cosmo had earlier been accused of kidnapping Ken
and hiding him in the basement. But my cherubic son had
denied the charge so extravagantly, so earnestly, that I had
stuck up for him and suggested that maybe Ken was merely
lost and that it wasn't right to make accusations without proof.

I said to Rocco, "I think it was recently attached to my
daughter's Ken doll. You know, Barbie's boyfriend." I smiled
ingratiatingly. Perhaps Rocco would find this amusing, and
smile back. But he did not.

"I don't know about Ken," he said. "But this was wedged
in there but good."

"Oh," I said.

In a roundabout way, Cosmo later did own up to flushing
Ken's leg down the toilet, but he clearly felt so justified in his
action that I could not be very angry, and besides, it seemed
better not to delve too deeply into his psychic rationale.
Winnie had always considered Ken an inferior specimen
anyway, missing, as he was, some essential male parts. Nor
could she stay angry very long with her little brother, and
there the matter rested.

Until the toilet flooded again.

With the wisdom of hindsight, of seeing the whole picture, you and I know what was found to be causing this new stoppage. But at the time there was no pattern yet, and so after failing in all the usual attempts at home plumbing, I called upon the Pentimenti brothers. This time Dominic came. It turned out that whatever was wrong was far, far along the pipe pathways, and the hydraulic snake was necessary. Cosmo watched intently as Dominic fed the coiled metal tubing into the maw of the toilet bowl; even his breathing seemed to keep time with the piston thump of the generator. Then Dominic put the pump into reverse and rewound the snake, and emerged from the bathroom with a small plastic limb, an arm upon closer examination. By then Cosmo had disappeared.

We all know what happened next. I tried to appear casual, even mildly amused, as if every family should expect to find flushed body parts in their plumbing. Dominic was laconic. Winnie referred to her brother as Rodent-boy, which interestingly enough, is the one name that stuck for the next fifteen-odd years.

Ken's other leg was flushed down about a week later but I managed to get it out myself with the aid of a reconfigured wire coat hanger, and thereby avoided calling in the Pentimenti brothers. By then it was clear to us that there remained at large other body parts, precisely, another arm, a torso, and a head, if memory of that poor unappreciated Ken served me correctly. Surely Cosmo knew where these body parts were while the rest of us did not.

The next time the toilet flooded I actually thought about trying to call in a new plumber, one unacquainted with our family history for flushing limbs. But it is impossible to get a new plumber to come, and the toilet was overflowing, so Rocco came by at the end of the day. This time it was Ken's left leg, that pathetic flat-footed specimen.

Rocco said, "I know it's none of my business, but maybe you should get him a toy of his own."

"Really?" I said. I was startled to be getting parenting advice, rather than plumbing advice, from Rocco. But why not? Didn't he have another life when he was not a plumber but a father? It seemed to me that we needed any words of wisdom that came along.

"Yeah. A GI Joe."

"I'd never thought of that," I said. "Do his limbs come apart, or is he all one piece?"

"That I don't know," Rocco said.

It was Dominic who came and unclogged my kitchen sink while Gus was serving aces at tennis camp. He had to take the hydraulic snake down to the basement and open up one of the mains. He said it took him three passes with the snake, that's how resistant the blockage was.

"But why?" I asked. "What could it be?"

"Looks just like sludge to me," he said.

"What is sludge? Is that in the eye of the beholder?" I said.

"Sludge is just what's no longer recognizable," Dominic said.

"Yes, I can see that. But is it more one thing than another? Is there something that shouldn't be going down there that is going down there?"

Clearly I wanted from Dominic some kind of reassurance

that he wasn't prepared to offer, not that he should have. Standing there in my lovely kitchen, where there is equal space given to Scrabble dictionaries and fondue dishes, the question of what people put down their kitchen drains was ever-present, and simultaneously, untouchable, taboo.

Dominic said, "Oh I doubt it. Everyone gets sludge. You just have some long and very old and windy pipes down there."

Because he had come so recently and unclogged the sink that first time Gus went away, to Amsterdam, Dominic did not charge me for the visit, or the unclogging. This was their policy, he said, as if the reclogging was somehow the responsibility of the Pentimenti brothers, and not the voice of my house and my life, and my kitchen. But I did not disabuse him of that fact, and was grateful.

The third time Gus went away, to the Erotica Convention in Philadelphia, the kitchen sink did not back up, and I was pleased, and not a little surprised. Not that I would have said such things aloud. I was superstitious about bad things happening in threes, and ever fearful of tempting the gods, even unwittingly, with hubristic satisfactions. The very next morning I was going into the local hospital to have the ganglionic cyst on my right wrist removed. I had suggested that Gus stay around and drive me to the hospital and drive me home, and he had suggested that I reschedule the surgery, since the Erotica Convention certainly was not about to be rescheduled for a bump on my wrist.

I draped myself on the cruciform operating table and stretched my arms out horizontally on the aprons that extended to either side. I said, "Tell me, was this table designed specifically for hand surgery?"

"Right," said the OR nurse.

"And I'm sure I'm not the first one to point out the uncanny resemblance to a certain shape, a certain icon of Western Civilization?"

She said, "Right, you're not."

The anesthesiologist hooked me up to the IV and then inserted a very large needle into my right armpit. "You'll feel a prick," he said. "And then you shouldn't feel anything at all."

The other nurse, a young man, said, "So, how did you get this cyst? Do you use your hand a lot?"

"Well I use it for writing. That's more or less all I do." That wasn't remotely true. I did many things more than I wrote. But just then I either forgot them or didn't want to admit to them. It was very cold in there. It was like being in the meat locker at Fairway. No, it wasn't *like* anything. It *was* being in a meat locker.

"What do you write?"

"Fiction. Nothing real, or true. Except that it all ends up being true. What I mean is, I believe that good fiction is essentially true, that is, true to human nature or the human condition, in a way that nonfiction isn't, not necessarily, because theoretically it is factual and the notion that facts exist is very fictive. I think." This was surely more than the nurse wanted to know. I sensed that if it were not for the Valium in my veins I would have clammed up and had a panic attack. Instead, I said, "Have the drugs kicked in yet? Am I talking a lot?"

"Give it time."

"I just feel like I'm rambling," I said. "I don't usually ramble."

"So what writers do you like?"

Suddenly this was the hardest question in the world, and it seemed so important that I not misspeak. But all the names of all the writers I'd ever loved fled from my brain; I was watching them scatter and depart my skull, with the urgency of rabbits and deer fleeing a forest fire. I squeezed out: "Virginia Woolf, Proust, Nabokov, Melville, Samuel Beckett, Balzac." Much as I loved all those writers I felt that my answer was deficient, that something else was demanded of me. I added: "Isak Dinesen, Lewis Carroll."

"Do you write romances?"

"No."

"Have you read Danielle Steele?" said one nurse.

"No," I said. I was still trying desperately to picture my bookshelves. How could I not have said Thomas Mann, or Jane Austen? Or Thomas Bernhard or Trollope? Or had I said their names?

"I read everything by Tom Clancy," said the other.

"Oh," I said.

Then the anesthesiologist pulled a book from his back pocket or perhaps from some secret niche in the operating theater. "Have you read this?" he asked me.

"I can't see. You guys took away my glasses," I said.

"That's terrible," he said, as if this were not the most standard of hospital procedures. "We'll send someone to get them for you."

"Great—you mean I'll actually get to see the surgery?"

"Viola, can you send someone to get her glasses?"

I told her exactly where they were, and she unpinned the locker key from my hospital bracelet.

His book was the new novel by Michael Ondaatje, which I had read but knew I was about to confuse it with something else. I said, "My favorite of his is the memoir of growing up in Ceylon. Back when it was Ceylon. Did you know that some people think Ceylon was the site for the Garden of Eden? I assume because it's so beautiful, and lush. There's a certain tropical fruit that is supposed to have been the apple Eve nibbled on, called cherimoya. Some people think it should be durian, but I'm pretty sure it's cherimoya. And there's a crater there called Adam's Footprint, or maybe it's a mountain called Adam's Nose."

"I'd never heard that," the anesthesiologist said.

"Probably because I made it up," I said. "Not that I made it up on purpose, but I have a tendency to say things as true—because I really think they are true, because I remember them quite vividly as true, and then it turns out I must have dreamed it all. Or had a déjà vu."

The surgeon then came in and asked me if I could feel anything in my right arm.

"Nothing, absolutely nothing," I said. "At least I think I feel nothing. Maybe I'm feeling something but I don't know it."

"Marvelous," he said. *"Merveilleux."* Dr. Jacques Citroen was from Lebanon and spoke French, which was probably why I'd picked him from a list of orthopods in the HMO Handbook. It hadn't occurred to me at the time, but there in the arctic operating theater it was as obvious as the bump on the wrist (my own little Krakatoa). I always went for doctors with accents. My very first psychiatrist was an unintelligible but beautifully dressed Italian countess, and then there was my handsome and soothingly paternal German gynecologist and of course my beloved Chilean psychiatrist with one leg. He was younger than I am now when he died suddenly, one summer in Martha's Vineyard. Until then I had thought it was an exaggeration to say that all psychiatrists went to Martha's Vineyard in August, but it turns out to have been true.

"So you're a writer," Dr. Citroen said, or I thought that was what he said. This unnerved me because I preferred to think he knew who I was and what I did, and also because it seemed terribly presumptuous to have called myself a writer when I had just trilled the names of my literary pantheon. Then I was afraid that he thought I was someone else who needed some other form of surgery. An amputation, perhaps? Should I have taken a Magic Marker and written strong prohibitions against lopping-off on all my pertinent limbs. *Not this arm! Not even this hand! Just this little cyst!*→ I looked over to see what was happening to the right wrist that I could feel not at all, but there was a curtain draped just above my shoulder to keep me from viewing.

"I've always wanted to go to Baalbek," I told him.

"Of course," he said. Perhaps he was doing something to my wrist. Perhaps not. I could feel nothing at all.

"My mother used to go to Beirut to get her clothes

made," I said. I was thinking of all those cocktail dresses
with matching jackets in brocades shot through with
golden and silver threads, those sculpted but flimsy artifacts
of that other life she led, growing up in Egypt, picnicking on
pyramids and collecting parasites. She no longer wore the
dresses. She shunned cocktail parties these days. Her back-
bone curved the wrong way and made it impossible to wear
high-heeled shoes, like Barbie; and cocktail dresses without
high-heeled shoes were as unseemly as the arctic without
ice. Now I keep her dresses in labeled garment bags in my
attic, awaiting another lifetime. "She said Beirut was the
Paris of the Middle East."

"It still is," said Dr. Citroen. This was confusing. Hadn't
there been a terrible civil war over there?

Time passed, and then he said, "Mon Dieu, this was quite
a tenacious cyst."

"You have it there? May I see it?" I said.

And there emerged from behind the curtain at my armpit
a small piece of bloody flesh dangling from the end of a
hemostat. It was tiny, smaller than a game hen's heart. I
didn't say that. Nor did I mention to them how pleased I was
to see it. After having had assorted tumors removed and
then whisked away to pathology while I was remained under
general anesthesia, this opportunity to actually see the
offending piece of flesh, this growth that I had grown, however unintentionally, this was almost a thrill. It would have
been a thrill were I not drugged.

"I was hoping to take it home," I said.

"I'm afraid you can't do that," Dr. Citroen said.

"Yes, I know that's what they say," I said. "Because I always ask, and they always say they can't release human tissue. But this is so little."

"And why do you want this, this cyst?" the anesthesiologist said.

"Because it's mine. I thought my kids might like to see it, and even if they'd rather not—was going to put it in this little spice jar, and float it in blue water. I've had this little jar for quite a while, and it's still empty," I said.

"You could just go to the butcher," the anesthesiologist said.

Then I was in the dream tunnel again. But as soon as I crawled back to something, not quite awakeness, in the recovery room, I recalled that butcher remark, and it bothered me. Then I became panic-stricken. Perhaps I hadn't said anything remotely akin to what I thought I had said, and had not gotten across what seemed to me a rather benign longing to hang on to my body parts, however insignificant, which was why he had made the comment about going to the butcher. It was hard to know.

I looked for my arm off to my right side, but it wasn't there. It was somewhere else, on top of the blanket, somewhere I hadn't put it at all. There was no feeling in the whole arm south of the armpit. The nothingness seemed very like having no arm at all, if I knew what such a thing felt like, which I did not. I pinched the completely flaccid bicep, and levered it up by the elbow: deadweight. I wondered how much an arm, unconnected to a body, might weigh. Mine in particular. I thought *This is just like having been amputated.* Or was it? As far as the weight went, wasn't it more like a paralysis, a total a-sensibility? But it was the sense of its not being there that overwhelmed me. I considered the grammar: Am I the one being amputated? Or would it be my arm that is amputated? For the amputee, the verb, to amputate, must always be in the passive tense. Or must it?

Dr. Citroen came in to see me. I wondered if I should speak French with him, if he would like me better if I did, if my scar would be smaller?

"So how do you feel?" he said.

"Not very much," I said. "Look—the whole arm is still numb. More than numb. Not yet there. Is this what it feels like when one is amputated? When one's arm is amputated?" I was still obsessing about what would be the correct object of that passive construction, grammatically speaking.

"Mais oui, it is something like that. Although in the case of amputation there is no arm."

"I know that," I said. "When can I go home?"

"As soon as you can feel something."

Having nothing else to do, I asked for more tranquilizers and dozed off again until I was woken up by an itch on my forearm. I reached down to scratch it, but the arm wasn't there again, wasn't where I thought it was, again. It had fallen off the side of the bed, like blankets after a turbulent dream. This was definitely like having been amputated. I looked for someone with whom to share this revelation, but the room was empty and unlit. For how long had I slept?

Later my friend Molly came to collect me and take me home.

She wanted to see the incision, but it was tightly bandaged up, from my fingertips to halfway up my forearm.

"You mean you haven't seen it either?" she said.

"No," I said. "I must have been Valium'd out during that part. But watch this." I lifted my right arm up with my left arm, and then let it drop. "It's dead weight," I said. "Have you ever wondered what your arm weighs? If you could weigh your body parts separately?" I could hear myself saying this again and again, trying it out on different people until someone stopped me with the actual information about the weight of an arm.

"I've never given it much thought," Molly said.

Outside, it was twilight, dusk, that almost darkness, that Proustian time. In her car, Molly said to me, "Just kiss him and he'll calm down. He's used to riding shotgun." Her brown furry dog, whose name changed every week, from Zelly to Marx to Samson, was squirming on my lap, wetly demanding attention and affection.

"This is just what it's like when you've been amputated," I said. "Even to the phantom limb pain. I have phantom limb itch."

"But you still have an arm," Molly said.

"This is true."

Left to my own devices at home, I placed my arm on the kitchen table and lightly dragged the tines of a fork over the skin and the bandages. Nothing. Then, emulating the infamous Chinese water torture, I dripped orange juice from a teaspoon onto my fingers. Nothing. Nothing, that is, except that I now had to be sure to bathe before becoming a sugary attraction for the ever-present ants. (Slow death by sweet-toothed ants being a Moroccan torture, if I remembered correctly.) Then I dropped on my forearm a volume of the OED, A-B, containing amputate, and arm, and anomaly. Surely this would be felt. And in a way it was, but not truly by the arm. I think it was the rest of me sensing the jiggling of the table from the five-pound tome that thudded upon it.

As the night progressed, feeling came back. Like Lazarus, but of course very different. The next day Gus came home, but by then I had feeling up and down my arm and the wrist was very sore. He said my understanding of the nature of amputation was all wrong.

"How can I have it wrong? It's not nuclear physics. Either you have a limb, or you don't."

"Amputation is about cutting off a diseased limb or body part, it's not about numbness."

"I know that," I told him. I asked him how the Erotica Convention had been. Actually I referred to it as a Porn Fest, and he was annoyed and started once again to berate me with the difference between pornography and erotica, which I considered specious, and he considered a moral imperative, and the conversation quickly disintegrated.

Later that day I unwound the bandages and was shocked at the length of the scar, a jagged cut across the wrinkles of my wrist. It looked as if I had tried to kill myself but extremely incompetently, having entirely missed the main artery.

I described all this to Winnie on the telephone. "It could be very embarrassing at dinner parties, with strangers thinking that I've tried to kill myself. That I'm mentally unstable. As well as being clueless about basic anatomy."

"But Mom, look at the bright side. Now you finally have a scar you can show off. Unlike your belly one." This was a point I had not considered.

Then later, I said to Gus, "It's becoming clear to me that tumors and growths and bumps and lumps are all psychosomatic, or least they're outgrowths of mental states. There is definitely a subtext here."

"I can't believe you're finally figuring this out," he said.

For days afterwards I would have fleeting moments of recalling the complete numbness in my arm and wishing for that sensation, that lack of sensation, back again, in order to test its absolute limits. When I'd had the chance, I should have continued, with hot water, with a brick, with thorny branches from the wild roses. I should have weighed it, and immersed it in ice water. I should have drawn blood. There had been this brief window in which to learn the difference between what I could really feel and what I only thought I could feel, and I had barely used it.

Lost in the Mail

This all happened more or less right after I had returned from a weekend at the Monastery of the Seven Brothers and Saint Felicity, a tiny retreat in the wilds of the Catskills populated by three rather old nuns, one of whom was on a retreat somewhere else, presumably somewhere even more remote, so that when I was there, there were only two elderly nuns.

I went there for at least two reasons, really three reasons. The first was to give thanks for the apparently miraculous disappearance of the olive-sized lump in my friend's breast. The second was to pray, in that place of silence, for my five-year-old niece with a *hamartoma,* a tumor on her hypothalamus that caused severe seizures, seizures every minute, seizures that built on each other until they were called a seizure storm.

I wanted to pray for Sadie more purely than I had hitherto managed, when I'd been seduced by the very language of the disease. When she'd first been diagnosed, I had gone straight to the OED to learn the roots of *hamartoma.* The suffix, *toma,* of course means a tumor, any tumor, all sorts of tumors. I already knew that. It was the *hamar* part that surprised me, and thus gave me the little frisson I always get when I discover a new word or unravel a particularly lively etymological puzzle. *Hamartia,* from the Greek, is the fault or error that entails the destruction of the tragic hero. *Hamartia* is the tragic flaw. It struck me as egregious, and cruel, to have named a tumor that way, a tumor that a baby could be born with. And if *hamartia* were not grim enough, then there was the root, *hamart,* meaning sin. *Hamartiology* is the doctrine of sin, the part of theology that treats of sin. It all shocked me: that such a thing as a doctrine of sin could exist, and that in all my years of obsessed hagiographic researches I had never come across it, and, worst of all, that I had forged right ahead and explained all this to Sadie's parents. Why had I felt so compelled? Clearly, if they already knew the etymology, then they knew, and if they didn't, they didn't need to. It occurred to me this could be a useful bit of crossword knowledge. (Clue: *hamartialogist's study.* Answer: sin).

Nor was this my first foray into medical, biographical, etymological studies. I had had my own tomas. These had been *teratomas,* from the Greek *terato,* for monstrous formations or births, and in fact they'd been periodically removed, leaving only the pattern of fading cicatrices. Even back then I was guilty of sharing with everyone who cared to know the Greek word, *teratos,* that meant a marvel, a prodigy, a monster. An intriguing triad? I postulated aloud, but only to Hildegard, my cumbrous slouching bulldog. Then I might venture into teratology, a discourse or narrative concerning prodigies; a marvelous tale, or collection of such tales. None of this struck me as remotely accidental, or random, or even idiopathic, as Dr. von Pfefferlingel had characterized my teratomas. Once you knew the language, it seemed painfully clear and intentional.

So if I was to pray for Sadie's health, for her parents' forbearance, I also had to pray that I could learn how to pray without parsing every sentence and dissecting every word, without relishing liturgy at the expense of piety.

And that led to the understory, the subtext of why I was at the monastery, which was to silently pace the surrounding forest and wonder if there was any chance that I could ever be a decent (not good, just decent) Catholic, when my greatest interest was in hagiography, hardly the most theologically elevated aspect of the church. According to some it was the most debased. And of hagiography, it was the weirder, and more ghoulish, and miraculous saints that I preferred: the virgin martyrs, the cross-dressers, the cephalophores, the incorrupt bodies. Each morning I read the day's entry in Butler's *Lives of the Saints,* and if I discovered a new one I felt somehow justified in my obsession, because it had borne fruit; such as today's Saint Maxellindis, another determined spinster whose intended bridegroom, Harduin, was struck blind when he dragged her from the linen chest where she was hiding and killed her with his sword. Later, the not-bridegroom Harduin's sight was miraculously restored when, lamenting, he fell on his knees by Maxellindis's coffin and vigorously mourned.

Just a few days ago I came across Saint Theoctista, whose story the hagiographers say is just an "empty fable." But

don't they always say that nowadays? Why should the latter-
day primary-source-obsessed historiography be any more
valid than early medieval legendizing? Theoctista was an
anchoress in the desert, feeding herself on fruits and vegetables for thirty years. When she was found by a man named
Simon, she had to hide in the bushes and yell out: "Don't
come any closer. I am a woman and I would be ashamed to
be seen by you, for I am naked." Later, when they came back
with the Eucharist in a pyx, they found her almost dead. She
died soon thereafter. Before she was buried Simon severed
one of her hands to take away with him as a holy relic. But
his ship refused to leave the port until he had restored the
hand, and when he did, it grew again onto the wrist.

I was especially intrigued to learn of the ship refusing to
sail with the hand onboard, because of the story of the Virgin
of El Viejo in Nicaragua. She too refused to sail out of the
harbor, repeatedly, and is an object of veneration in Chinan-
dega, Nicaragua. Because, as will be seen, there is in this narrative a recurring motif of intransigent Virgin statues.

In the forest behind the monastery I peeled birch bark
from the trees and wrote messages, about Sadie, and my
friend's lump, even some limericks. The limericks were,
unfortunately, very bad. They always are. I have always
loved writing on birch bark. The returned pressure of the
bark against the nib of the pen suggests a response, a
willing participant in the written, an equal pleasure in
being written upon. Then I frightened a huge buck, an
enormous buck with antlers reaching for the sky, certainly
the biggest buck I have ever been close to. I couldn't

understand why he leaped away—and what a leap—upon hearing my insignificant leaf-rustling. Then I thought, *Of course, it's hunting season. This is a stag with the hardwired memory of his kind.*

When I got home my daughter, Winnie, called with a request. She asked me if I had any books about sex and specifically about masturbation, and because I have books about almost everything and indeed, books about sex, I sent her three well-chosen tomes.

"Are we talking about self-help manual-type books here?" I asked at first.

"Mom! You know I learned all that stuff in middle school. Remember Sex-Ed. When Miss Rhubarb had us say the word penis one hundred times in order to demystify it."

"I don't remember her saying anything about demystification back then," I said.

"She didn't," Winnie said. "But I have since gained some insight into her pedagogical technique."

Winnie was at college working on an art installation that promised to be interesting. And very likely more revealing and risqué than anything with which I would be comfortable. But that wasn't the point. There was soon to be a reception to which she planned to invite all her relatives, that is, her four grandparents, her nine aunts, her seven uncles, and her twenty-four first cousins, and I wasn't sure how my mother-in-law would like graphic, if very artistic, depictions of sex techniques. But I was probably putting the cart before the horse. Chances were by the time Winnie was finished it would all be transformed into some wonderfully abstract and patterned construction.

I sent her three books. The first, Masters and Johnson's *Human Sexual Response,* I had several copies of, because it shows up at every used book sale I have ever attended. I know this because I always check at book sales, first to make sure the book is there, and then to see if there are any interesting marginalia. The second book was called something like *The Technology of Orgasm,* but it was really about the invention of the vibrator in the early twentieth century. Apparently, battery-powered vibrators were introduced as an aid to the doctors who used them to relieve their frustrated patients. There was actually more about engineering than about sex in the book, but it seemed pertinent enough to Winnie's subject.

But my favorite was always *Sexology,* published in 1909 by the Puritan Publishing Company. I had found the book in the attic when we moved to this house many years ago, and from the very first I had known it was a treasure. Although it had been a long time since I had read it, I remembered certain sections well; and besides, they were easy to find since I had marked them with wispy pieces of paper. So I could steer Winnie straight to the most lurid, and, to our advanced modern sensibilities, the most shocking anecdote. It was in a chapter entitled "Masturbation, Female: The Horrors Thereof," and it described the case of a young girl in France. I have noticed that these things always happen in France, at least in American books they do. She was apparently in ill health and the doctor called in, an expert in ailments of little girls, maintained this was due to her having engaged in the "most wicked of vices." But he could not prevail on the girl, a mere eleven years old, to admit to the crime. So he persuaded her mother to send her to the countryside to live alone with a crabby old aunt, where he could badger her daily with the same question, until she admitted to the wicked deed. Which of course she finally did, but by then, the story went, it was too late and her health was irretrievably gone.

I put all three books into a large padded mailing envelope and wrote Winnie a note on the back of a postcard with a photograph of a bulldog wearing sunglasses sitting on a beach under a striped umbrella. When they were away from home I always sent my children cards with bulldogs on them, because I knew how they missed Hildegard, and I worried how they slept at night without the obbligato of her canine snoring.

Later that week I walked down the hill from my house, kicking with pleasure at the fallen oak and maple and even the gigantic sycamore leaves, the leaves on steroids, and went to a lecture about Hildegard von Bingen. The notice about it in our local paper had been in extremely small print, giving rise to the suspicion that attendees were not really required or even wanted. But still I went.

I went not just because I named my bulldog, Hildy, for her, the 12th-century visionary, composer, writer, and saint, although that would have been enough, certainly, on a resplendent, shimmering Saint Jude's Day. I went for the same reason I read Butler's *Lives of the Saints,* and visited monasteries, and preferred to attend mass in foreign languages, because even as I found testimony of mystical experiences and visions compelling, I was skeptical, and I wanted to be purged of skepticism.

The lecture was specifically about Hildegard von Bingen's music, which was lovely: the music, not the lecture, which was almost nonexistent. Its most pronounced characteristic was the speaker's use of the word *extraordinary* no less than eighteen times in about thirty minutes. I documented this iteration by means of tics on the side of my program, four tics and then a horizontal slash to bundle up that bunch, and then on to the next five. And it is safe to assume that she, the lecturer, said *extraordinary* at least three times before I noticed its so frequent occurrence, and decided to keep track.

"What was *extraordinary* was Hildegard's young age when her mystical experiences began. She was five."

It is not unheard of for me to count things and especially word usage. I do it for agendas and menus and thank-you notes and grant proposals. Countless are the church bulletins I have illustrated with the numbers of sneezes in the congregation during the sermon, or references to *stewardship,* or uses of the word *fellowship* as a verb, a particular bugbear of mine. What is unusual, however, is for a pattern to continue so emphatically once I begin my documentation, as it did at the Hildegard lecture, with the word *extraordinary.*

"For the sin of burying an excommunicated man, the entire monastery was punished by being denied the privilege of singing as well as the taking of the Eucharist, for six long months. This was an *extraordinary* loss for these cloistered nuns."

Perhaps what first called my attention to the word was the way she pronounced it, ex-straw-dinary, with that lengthened second syllable, like a sandwiched sheaf of straw that was stretched out like elastic and then illuminated. I thought it an odd, somewhat affected pronunciation. But when she had said the word in that same way, *ex-straw-dinary,* for the fifth or sixth time, I had to acknowledge that she meant to pronounce it this way. Then I wondered, what if I have been mispronouncing it all along? What if there IS a sheaf of straw in the middle of the word?

"If you consider how impressed we are that Wagner wrote the words and music for his operas, you can imagine how *extraordinary* it was for Hildegard, in the twelfth century, tucked away in a monastery, to be composing the music and writing the words of her sacred opera, *Ordu Virtutum.*"

Clearly, I would have to give more thought to Wagner. And then this happened, as I suppose it was bound to. I began to think of the meaning of the word. *Extra-ordinary.* Is that out-of-the-ordinary, which is to say unusual, exceptional, not the normal state of affairs at all, perhaps even a little bizarre? Or does it mean an extreme of ordinariness, more-ordinary-than-the-usual ordinary, the most normal, standard thing that could be possible? Of course I knew that the latter meaning was not correct, and never had been. But when you consider extra helpings of dessert, as in more of the same, then it does not seem far-fetched at all.

"The *extraordinary* symbolism of Satan being the only personage in the opera without a singing role is almost not worth mentioning."

I know now, after consultation with my beloved OED, what I didn't know while I sat at the lecture, that there is a musical, albeit obsolete definition of *extraordinary*, which is: accidental. And in optics there is something called an *extraordinary* refraction. And then in diplomacy we have the envoy *extraordinary*, for some reason in my experience always said in French, as in *l'ambassadeur extraordinaire.*

"It wasn't until the publication of her *extraordinary* book, *Scivias,* following upon her midlife crisis, that fame came to Hildegard."

But at the Hildegard lecture I didn't have the benefit of all those pounds of print, and all those years of lexicographical research, and I had to ponder the meaning for myself. My assumption was, and remained, that the lecturer's intent was to frame Hildegard as out of the ordinary, above and beyond ordinary, that her accomplishments were remarkable for a woman in her time—I might even say for any man or woman in any time. But what if that opposite, opposed meaning is allowed to seep in, just a bit? What if Hildegard, the Sibyl of the Rhine, was paradigmatic for the female monastic of her time? What if the monasteries of Saxony and Burgundy and Picardy and Alsace were full of scholarly and gifted nuns, in regular conversation with God and His mother and His saints? What if they were all in the habit of writing pithy letters to the king and the pope and the bishops and the empress, offering savvy political advice as well as spiritual wisdom?

"In her extraordinary letter to Bernard of Clairvaux, Hildegard describes her 'inner visions' and the misery they cause her, and asks him simply: What do you make of all this?"

Well, the lecturer was right about the letter to Bernard of Clairvaux. If *extraordinary* were not so debased, it would most certainly be *extraordinary*, also amazing, luminous, and moving. Hildegard wrote: "I will be so easily crushed by the falling wooden beams in the winepress of my nature, that heavy wood growing from the root which sprang up in Adam through Satan's influence and cast him out into the world where there was no fatherland." I would love to know how he responded, this pure Cistercian monk in his white linen habit, who instigated the disastrous Second Crusade, this miracle worker who excommunicated flies, a host of swarming flies all banished forever from the good Graces of Mother Church, he whom Hildegard addressed as "the eagle who gazes at the sun."

Winnie called the next morning as I was contemplating appropriate footwear for a lunch in the city. I knew I wanted to wear red shoes; it was a question of which red shoes, and how flat, and what I could get away with.

"Mom, how many books did you send me?" she asked.

"You mean the sex books?" I said. "I told you, there were the three of them."

"Well then something really weird has happened. Only two arrived."

"What do you mean only two arrived?"

"The package had been torn open and there were only two books in it," she said.

"Holy smokes. Maybe it ripped accidentally and one fell out in your mailbox," I said.

"No, Mom, take my word for it. It was ripped open and then sealed back up, only now there are two books inside."

"That is very creepy," I said. "Which two?"

I could hear the rustling of paper as Winnie looked. It was very strange to think of someone opening my package of well-selected sex books, and why. There had been nothing about the package to indicate the tasty treats that lay within, or so I thought.

"*Sexology* and *Human Sexual Response* are here," Winnie said.

"Oh my God," I said. "That means the one about the invention of the vibrator is gone. And I thought you would find it so entertaining."

"Were there pictures in it?" Winnie asked.

"As it happens, there were. Mostly reproductions of print advertisements for those clever devices," I said. "I hope someone in some post office is enjoying it. What if it was *our* post office? All the guys there know me."

Winnie said, "Well, now they know you even better."

"That's not funny," I said. "But at least they didn't take *Sexology*. I would have been heartbroken to lose *Sexology*."

"I hope you didn't underline a lot in that other book," Winnie said. "You have a bad habit of underlining almost everything in your books."

This was true. I did underline a lot, but I did not regard it as a bad habit.

Then I told Winnie about Ralphie's costume for Halloween. Ralphie was her godson, a funny child of seven who loved to dress up and was far too sweet for this world. For Halloween he had been Henry the Eighth, complete with colored tights, a pillow under his brocade waistcoat, a golden chain of office, and a velvet cape on which were listed the names of his six wives and their respective fates: Divorced, Beheaded, Died, Divorced, Beheaded, Died.

"Thanks, Mom," Winnie said. "That makes me feel much better." She wasn't kidding. "I really love that kid."

"Me too," I said. "Plus he loves my red shoes. I'm considering red shoes as we speak."

I decided on the scarlet pumps—very low pumps because my balance has never been very good—because that shade went best with the red shell I wore under the black wool suit, a particular favorite of mine. It was a Dolce & Gabbana I'd bought at deep discount a mere season too late. Just to pull it all together I wore garnet earrings. A subtle touch, I thought.

"Where are you going dressed like that?" Gus emerged from his lair as I was unearthing a set of keys.

"I told you," I said. "The Eco-dinner for Tatty Newnham."

"You never told me," he said.

"You just didn't listen," I said. Variations on this interchange occurred almost every day, things being what they were.

"I can't believe you're going dressed like that."

"What's wrong with the way I'm dressed?" I asked. I was crestfallen. It was a constant shock to me, how, after all these years of marital critique of my wardrobe, of its well-considered idiosyncrasies, of its cost, I still longed for his approbation, longed for him to enter a room and say, "Hey Babe, you look great."

That was not to be. He said, "You know that red and black are Satan's colors. You can't go to a holy event dressed up for Satan."

"I never said it was a holy dinner, and that's not remotely funny," I said.

"It wasn't meant to be funny—I'm trying to help you avoid offending God and his minions."

"I doubt that's what you're worried about. I'd love to linger here for you to trash my outfit, but the train leaves in five minutes." Then I power-walked down to the station and made the train to Grand Central, so I could attend a dinner at the Chasuble Club in honor of the Very Reverend Ignatius Newnham, and just in time too, because the very next day he dropped dead while masturbating. Perhaps, having close ties to the postal services, he'd been reading our missing book, *The Technology of Orgasm*. But that seems too far-fetched, even for me. And it was not exactly a fact that he was masturbating at the moment of death, it was merely a very well substantiated rumor, a rumor coming from as close to the horse's mouth as we were ever likely to get, the horse's nostrils perhaps.

But at the luncheon—which honored his achievements in saving farmlands upstate, farmlands that were also home to the pilgrimage site called Santa Maria Salinica, a salt cavern where a weeping statue of the Virgin was found, where she still is, because she refuses to go elsewhere— Tatty's imminent death was not even on the horizon.

Tatty and I had known each other, carnally as they say, back in college, before he had gone to Divinity School, not that any of us were surprised by his vocation. While our intimacy had been a brief fluke as his sexual preference was otherwise, our friendship was cemented by long afternoons spent wearing each other's clothes and drinking Pernod and reading aloud the poetry of William Blake. We had discovered in each other a matching passion for Blake's *Songs of Innocence and Experience*. It had happened one wintry afternoon in a senior seminar called "Outsider European Intellectual History, Post-Enlightenment, and the Beginnings of Mystical Individualism." Perhaps that wasn't exactly the seminar's title. But that's not the point. The point is that Tatty, apropos of who knows what, said, *"Little Lamb, who made Thee?"* and I replied, without considering the potential for embarrassment, *"He is called by thy name, For He calls himself a Lamb. He is meek & He is mild; He became a little child. I am a child & Thou a Lamb, We are called by his name."* Periodically, Tatty asserted that I was the one who queried, *"Little Lamb, Who Made Thee?"* and he the one who answered, and we often argued about the sequence of events, and the reliability of memory. Then years later, in a volte-face or almost one, he said that the instigatory poem was actually *The Clod and the Pebble*; he claimed that I said, *"Love seeketh not itself to please,"* and he followed with, *"So sung the little Clod of Clay,"* and thus was our friendship born. Why he changed not only the speakers but also the poem was a mystery to me.

It was in Divinity School that Tatty found his calling as an eco-soldier for God. Every few years we would see each other and drink Pernod, much less Pernod of late, and hold hands and thumb wrestle, and misremember poetry.

Not that we did anything of the sort at the Chasuble Club. At the CC he stood at the podium and explained the theological imperative for saving farmlands, and pronounced pollution to be a sin. We were all very moved.

I was seated at a distant table with several people I'd never met before. Polite conversation was never my strong suit. In my desperate desire to say something entertaining yet not offensive or oppositional, I usually wasted half the meal in internal critique of my potential remarks. Then on subsequent outings I would determine to do better, to jettison my essentially selfish hang-ups, and plunge into conversation as into bracing cold water. To which end, I turned to my dinner partner, whose place card asserted his name to be Rupert Framboise, and asked him if he believed in sin.

He turned to face me—and the better to notice his wandering left eye—and said, "If you mean original sin, I would have to admit that the jury is still out. But if you mean do I believe in sin as in the existence of evil, or more specifically, if I believe pollution is a sin in the sense that it is a desecration of the earth that is ours to enjoy and preserve, then the answer is yes. Was that your question?"

"I'm not sure," I said. "I mean, I don't think I'd thought it through to that extent. That's not true entirely. I was thinking of sin as the intention to do wrong. And how would that apply to pollution?"

"You're suggesting that unintentional pollution would not be sinful?" he said.

"Well, when you put it like that . . . in fact, I do worry about the problem of intent. I'm always afraid that I blame people too much for what they do unintentionally, innocently as it were."

"Like a guy who changes his oil on the weekends and pours the old stuff directly into the storm drain?"

"Something like that. Actually, that's an interesting example because it points to the question of sins by omission or commission. Is he pouring it into the storm drain with the intent of polluting the ground water? Or because he's too lazy to recycle? Or is it possible that he honestly thinks that that is an acceptable way to dispose of filthy used oil?" What had compelled me to start this conversation, of all possible conversational topics in the Tristate area? Because once started it was clearly a slippery slope upon which every unconscious or ill-conceived action (or inaction, of course) was subject to glaring scrutiny, which would reveal the whole fabric of my life as flawed. This man, this Rupert Framboise, with his endearing wandering eye, seemed far too sincere, too good-natured, to be the serendipitous object of my belated parochial school angst.

"Is it omission, or is it a question of gravity? Mortal or venial, as it were," Rupert said.

"You must be Catholic," I said, probably too eagerly. It's not as if we were an endangered species.

"Well, I was a long time ago. I'm afraid it's largely gone by the wayside."

"But does it ever?" I said. "You know, Tatty Newnham has some well-concealed subterranean Papist leanings. Or he did in his youth. When we shared an interest in hagiography."

"I had no idea," Rupert said.

"Not that scrutiny of the lives of the saints gets me any closer to figuring out the sin question."

"I don't see why not," Rupert said. "The saints were hardly sinless."

"You're right, of course. But sooner or later they all move into a largely sinless state, a state of Grace. And they all believed in sin, I think."

"I think there is much about what they believed we will never know."

"It may be time," I said, "to expand my studies from hagiography to hamartialogy."

I couldn't then, nor can I now, believe that I actually used that word, which I had clearly been longing to use in some way, in a conversation with a perfect stranger.

I took a bite of the chicken which I later learned was quail, which if I had been paying more attention to what was going into my mouth, I might have realized earlier, and if I'd been paying that kind of attention, I might not have choked and thus never spoken to Tatty again before he died.

But as if chewing vigorously and thoughtlessly could erase my conversational bathos, I so chewed, and the quail that was not chicken made its way down my windpipe where it was not meant to go, and I began to cough and the more I coughed the more it seemed there was less and less oxygen getting to my brain and more and more a likelihood of my spewing food right there in the Chasuble Club. Rupert looked concerned and asked if he should pat me on the back. I shook my head to dismiss his concerns, coughed again, and then, at last, fled the room. Not a moment too soon. In the Ladies Room I coughed and coughed and finally spat out the offending fowl flesh.

Where did quail fit into the arcana of sumptuary laws? I later wondered. I'd always appreciated the so-called Jesuitical reasoning that allowed Catholic prelates to eat beaver and otter on Fridays, because they also swam in the sea, and by such tortuous logic, could be defined as fish.

When I was at the Monastery of the Seven Brothers and Saint Felicity, it came to my attention that Hildegard of Bingen, like the two elderly nuns who resided there, had been a Benedictine. In the tiny kitchen of the retreat house, there was an enormous book about Saint Benedict, his life and miracles, featuring every instance of his appearance in the plastic arts. And since I was not a nun in a refectory being read aloud to from the *Lives of the Desert Fathers,* as Benedict laid down in his Rule, I read silently to myself and looked at pictures in this book as I ate the simple but wholesome monastery fare. I learned that among his many miracles, which included two resurrections, Benedict was known, and beloved, for curing Emperor Henry II of his kidney stones. I was interested because Gus, as well as several near and dear friends, had suffered through kidney stones and all evidence indicated that this was extremely painful. Women described it as being right up there with unmedicated childbirth; men described it as worse than childbirth. It is not clear how Benedict cured the tormented emperor, especially given that their lives were separated chronologically by four hundred twenty-six years.

In the carving by Riemenschneider on the tomb of Henry, the Saint is shown standing by the Imperial sickbed holding an object in his left hand that may be meant to be the kidney stone (in which case it should have been fatal) but in fact looks very like the head of a penis, an imperial penis. The naked Henry lies back on his pillow groaning either with relief or excruciating pain. We will never know which.

As soon as I saw that picture and read of the miracle, I longed to tell my friend Donald, who is a nephrologist blissfully obsessed with all the various stones within the human body, especially the beautifully named renal calculi. As he is Jewish, I did not expect him to believe, as a matter of faith, in Saint Benedict's cure, but as a natural healer I knew he would be intrigued by this Ur-alternative healing. I also looked forward to telling Gus.

"I'm not saying I know what Saint Benedict did, but maybe he would be an appropriate person to pray to for relief. As an intercessor, of course." Gus had started life as a Unitarian and still clung to that sect's New-Englandish principles of tolerance, a very peculiar form of tolerance; what he generally had to say about the saints was not worth repeating.

"I don't think you appreciate how painful kidney stones are," he said.

"I thought I was expressing that very appreciation," I said.

"You were trying to be amusing. Note the word: trying, not succeeding."

"Not amusing at all," I said. "I honestly thought you'd be interested. But just forget it."

"Do you know how painful stones are?"

"Of course I do. Who drove your agonized self to the ER? They're like childbirth."

"They're a lot worse than childbirth, and there's no reward at the end."

"There isn't for most things in life," I said. "Unless you care to regard going on in life as the reward. More of the same."

A few days later Winnie called. "Have I got news for you," she said.

"That's good," I said. "What is it?"

"Can't you guess?"

But I can never guess, as she well knew. I said, "The missing book was mysteriously returned. It was hidden inside a hollowed-out seventeenth-century edition of Vorigne's *Golden Legends* and hand-delivered to you by a cadaverous man wearing a black domino."

"A black what? Never mind. It's nothing to do with the book."

"Then what could it possibly be?"

"I got an animal."

I said, "As opposed to a vegetable or a mineral?"

Winnie said, only very mildly exasperated, "No, as a pet."

"You're making me nervous. Am I to assume that this is not a bulldog?"

"That's a given," she said. "Actually, it's not a mammal."

"I don't think I'm going to like what you say next," I said.

"But you don't have to live with him," she said.

"Well I'm glad *he* has an identifiable sex."

"I named him Iggy," she said. "Now can you guess?"

"Assuming it's not a pop star, where did you find an iguana? And where do you keep him?"

"My friend Sam is leaving the country for a couple of years and couldn't take him with him. And he's really cute and doesn't have to be walked and doesn't bark or snore or fart."

"But is he affectionate? Does he return your care with mute and unambiguous adoration?"

"As a matter of fact he does. Sam called him Thunderball, but I never liked that, and Iggy seems to prefer his new name."

"How can you tell?" I said.

Winnie wisely ignored me. "Plus he likes my music," she said.

"I'll send you a Hildegard von Bingen CD," I said.

"If it'll make you happy, Mom, but I don't think we'll be listening to it."

Later that day I got the call telling me of Tatty Newnham's sudden and shocking and uncalled-for demise. I wanted to weep but could not. Everything made me choke or think I was about to choke, as if I'd swallowed an iguana or had a tumor lodged in my throat or just was terribly sad.

The Merits of Bats

For C. H. R., with love

Even before Malone had actually died, his cousin Dennis wondered aloud what would happen to his pornography collection. He was not alone in this.

"Has he written a will?" Maureen asked.

"Why shouldn't he have a will? Don't we all have wills?" I said, too quickly.

"I was just wondering," Maureen said. She was Dennis's wife, an in-law like me. "Because he's so hard to understand."

"No reason," Dennis said.

My husband, Gus, said, "I'd like find out where it all is. I think he once told me he had that famous issue of *Penthouse* with what's-her-name in it. It's a collector's item."

"That depends on the collector, I imagine," I said.

Gus glared at me.

Malone was my cousin-in-law, which is probably no real relation at all. He was my husband's first cousin, a few years younger than us, the son of Gus's Uncle Basket and Aunt Prudence. They were the Christian Scientist side of the family, and devout. To someone like me brought up in the fraught and schizoid tradition of Belgian Catholicism, they were stranger than Hottentots. I'd never met a Christian Scientist before I married Gus. I suppose his relatives thought I was equally strange. One of his brothers explained to me, "It's not very Christian and it's certainly not Science."

Aside from the Christian Science, which descended down through Aunt Prudence's line, Malone might have been much like my in-laws, his Codwell relatives (all lapsed Unitarians), but for the compelling fact of spending all his adult life in a wheelchair and day by day losing control of his body. This gave him access to a mordant sense of humor that was way beyond the reach even of Gus and his numerous brothers, whose comedic talents had been forged in the fire of the Three Stooges.

Malone had a rare disease called Friedreich's ataxia which was incurable, or untreatable, or both. This disease caused progressive degeneration of the spinal cord and nervous system. Its sufferers rarely lived past their twenties. Malone was forty-two and had been in a wheelchair since his very late teens. During the years I had known him, he had gone from heroically lurching, to walking with a stick and hurling himself at the next piece of furniture, to the standard manually operated wheelchair and then through several generations of motorized wheelchairs up to his last one—which had been fitted with special wheels in order to negotiate the paths through the woods that linked the houses on the family camp where he now lived all year round (now that his parents had retired) and where all his cousins came in the summers.

Even with the special wheels—like the extra-fat tires on certain tractors to reduce soil compaction—he sometimes got stuck in low-lying sandy patches and skidded and spun the wheels helplessly. We got him an emergency high-pitched whistle to alert us to his plight, so that he might be rescued before being eaten alive by platoons of kamikaze mosquitoes.

In the summers he careened up and down the private road with deliberate and valiant unconcern for the cars that came too fast, almost always driven by one of his cousins or their teenage children learning to drive. Malone clung to whatever mobility he could manage, and took himself where no wheelchair had ever gone before. His greatest challenge was the long road to our house, the last unpaved outpost. It was difficult of access with slick oak leaves and huge gnarled roots that ribbed the dirt road like natural speed bumps. He was always trying to come upon me unawares, hoping, so he claimed, to repeat that occasion of once, long ago, when he emerged from the woods to find me shade-bathing topless, sleeping over Proust. I always read Proust in those summers.

In the long winters overlooking the salt marsh, Malone wrote science fiction in spurts and disparaged every page. He joined the Bat Conservancy and took every opportunity to speak well of those maligned mammals, not rodents as he often pointed out. He said he identified with them, because of the revulsion they provoked. He wasn't kidding. As we scratched ourselves bloody from insect bites he reminded us that a single brown bat could eat twelve hundred mosquitoes in one hour. If that boon to humanity could not inspire affection, then what could?

He was also an incurable romantic, loved several women, and longed for sex. He read and collected pornography, and was cavalier about it in a way that would have been unacceptable in anyone else, in anyone not stuck in a wheelchair and fading fast. When he discovered the Internet and found the triple-X sites, his room down the road became a pilgrimage site for the teenage cousins. There was a certain amount of parental upset among the relatives and in-laws. But no one would ever ream him out for inappropriate behavior, as they would have anyone else setting such a bad example; Malone understood immunity and what it signified, and he chose to relish it.

Only by dint of extreme effort and constant therapy could Malone hang on to what little control he had of his extremities. The feet and legs went first. They atrophied and became weights that he struggled to shift in his wheelchair; in the summer his feet swelled terribly and became so purple they almost glowed. He could not move them but they could cause him pain. Then it was his arms and hands. He said his butt was chronically sore. His speech grew distorted and even with an operation to put a steel rod in his spine, his torso kept collapsing on itself and his head was always tilted.

Malone and I had carried on a passionate correspondence for almost twenty years, since the early days of my marriage. All that time he wrote me lewd, self-deprecatory missives, brilliant and bizarre in their lack of connection to any life that I was living at the time. Or perhaps not. After one lovely humid summer he wrote me:

> *"We all have our secrets. Mine are tattooed in Braille on my thighs.*
> *Care to read them sometime?"*

In the last two years, our correspondence went from being sporadic to being totally one-sided. Malone had lost the use of his fingers and couldn't even type on his enhanced keyboard.

But back in the early days he once wrote thus, responding to my very first computer-written letter:

> *"I have a passion for giving unwanted advice that is rivaled only by my passion for viewing naked women during their most intimate and private encounters, and I noticed what a heavy impression your obviously dot-matrix printer was making—not too good as this wears out your ribbon as well as your printhead."*

Another time he wrote:

> *"I was impressed, awed, thrilled, speechless (not very likely) delighted and . . . Your last letter really floored me, figuratively, of course. I mean it's such a royal bitch to get me up off the floor once I get down there that I tend to avoid tonguing the rug whenever physically feasible . . . do you blame me?"*

I had no idea what I had written to him.

As Malone deteriorated, so did all his epistolary relationships deteriorate to the holiday sending of Hallmark cards, which his mother, Aunt Prudence, unfortunately chose for him.

For many years I refused to accept the obvious fact—to which I have finally reconciled myself—that there is an altogether different physical sensation on the plane trip home than on the plane trip out. On the away plane trip I can actually watch my hands not shake. I make lists, eat nuts and dried fruit, and read illuminating books. Then I fall asleep with ease. Whereas on the going-home trips there is the problem that I attract weird fundamentalist types who first sit next to me, and then tell me what missionary activity they've lately engaged in, specifically what encroachments they've made in the good fight against the Papist AntiChrist, that idolatrous menace. I never feel more Catholic than when I encounter a fundamentalist Protestant. They make me wish I was wearing a large graphic and baroque crucifix. They make me wish I had a handy and portable reliquary, containing the finger bones of Saint Christina the Astonishing or some hair of Saint Winifred.

There is something tangibly different about flying north or west that makes me fearful of mid-ocean crashes and toxic air quality and where my children are at that exact moment and whether my asthmatic, lame bulldog will have survived the kennel or died of fright, as so many of her predecessors have done. On the going-home trips I suffer from anxiety and spleen even as I am anticipating my own sheets and my own lumpy down pillows.

On the last flight across the Atlantic I was reading the cartoon version of Proust's *Recherche du temps perdu,* which was not as easy to do as it sounds. For one thing, French was not my first language. In order to even remove the brightly colored book from my satchel, I had to struggle with the potential embarrassment of being seen by some person or persons I didn't know then nor would ever know, seen reading what looked like a children's book. It should have been enough that I knew it was not a children's book; it should not have mattered what my fellow passengers thought I was reading; nor was it remotely likely that they would care.

None of that has ever alleviated my anxiety. Why should reality intervene? The first thing I do whenever I see someone else reading on a plane or train is decipher the title, and based on whatever little knowledge I possess of that title and author I then leap to all sorts of judgments and impressions of the unsuspecting reader. This unproductive and distracting tendency to make hasty and ill-considered judgments based on almost no information may go back to an incident that occurred when I was much younger. A famous and extremely good-looking writer once sat next to me on a plane and set out to seduce me because, so he said, I was reading *The Magic Mountain* at the time. I remember the book very well: it was from the public library in the tiny town in northern New Hampshire where I had been working that summer and it was the first time I had ever taken a library book on an airplane with me. It felt like a very daring thing to do. I had given serious thought to the question of taking it along and had pondered who would be responsible for the library fines if the plane disappeared into the frigid thalassic darkness, along with me and *The Magic Mountain*.

That incident may be the source of this obsessive need to know what others are reading, but it probably is not. I suspect it goes back farther than that, to some seminal childhood experience that only analysis could unearth.

I thought I was flying home to snowbound New York and then driving north to visit Malone, who was hitched up to respirators and given less than six months to live. Given is an odd word choice, or perhaps not, all of life being a gift.

I was hoping very much to say good-bye to Malone, and also personally deliver to him some extremely sexy postcards I had bought in France. But he died, in pain, not long after my plane hit the runway.

A few years ago, he wrote me this letter:

"I wanted to assure you that I haven't died. I mean, I'm not dead. At least, I don't think I am. Put it this way: no one has thrown dirt on my face for quite some time. The Coke keeps disappearing from my fridge. And since I'm the only one around here who drinks the stuff I suppose that means there is still some semblance of life left in these old bones. Not much, I grant you, but enough. For what I use it for there's more than enough."

There was no forgetting imminent mortality when I was with Malone, but I seemed to ignore it all the same. Later that year he wrote:

"They say absence makes the heart grow fonder. Are you fond of me yet? I'm sorry I've been so remiss in my 'meaningful' correspondence with you of late, dear lady. But you know better than most just what

type of doggie refuse I am. . . . . I've run out of clever ways to say I've been doing naught in these troubled times but produce a veritable mountain of belly-button lint. I'd cry, but my glasses would probably turn green. . . . . Of course the giant slug that's been following me around for the past couple of weeks hasn't exactly inspired me, either. Can you imagine what it's like to have two tons of invertebrate slime breathing down your neck to play Chutes 'n' Ladders at all hours of the day or night?"

In the west-bound plane when my concentration on Proust waned, and anxiety took over, I obsessed about Johnny and Luther Htoo, the chain-smoking, twelve-year-old twins from Burma. They had nothing at all to do with my life. Myanmar, as it was now called, lamentably, was almost as far away from New York as one could get (the actual farthest place still on this planet was somewhere in the arid middle of Australia) and had I gotten there I would have been unable to read one single word in the Indic Burmese script. I had seen it on a tube of incense, and it looked to me like rows of soap bubbles in boxes. I could not distinguish a consonant from a vowel, or a subject from a predicate. Johnny and Luther were leaders of a splinter group of ethnic Karen rebels, called God's Army. Sometime in the past month, they had taken eight hundred hospital patients hostage, in Thailand. I had read about them in the *Herald-Tribune* but there had been no photograph and so I inserted the charmed twelve-year-old face of my son, Cosmo, into the larger picture of a terrorized hospital in Southeast Asia. Cosmo was no longer twelve but he was still charmed. I pictured the patients in hospital-issue sarongs pleading for morphine and water while the twin boys chain-smoked and proselytized.

Johnny and Luther were fundamentalist Christians; they believed they had mystical powers that made them safe from bullets and land mines.

Where was their mother all this time? I kept wondering. The part about feeling invulnerable was easier to understand. After all, what did twelve-year-olds know? What had Winnie and Cosmo known back then? What did I know when I was twelve? Far far less than any of them. And no twelve-year-old boy I've ever known has ever believed that he was mortal and subject to the same laws of nature that ruled his clueless parents. Which is why my brother Gabriel chopped off his thumb with a hatchet, and why my brother James got frostbite on seven of his ten fingers on a winter camping trip in New Hampshire, and why my brother Olivier broke his tibia in four places when he considered a career as a funambulist and practiced on the peak of the barn roof. Gabriel's thumb was reattached. Frostbite turns black and then green and then eventually goes away, even if James is forever after extra-sensitive to cold in those seven digits. Broken legs reset and are usually stronger than they were before, especially in twelve-year-olds. But none of that applies to land mines.

And not only did Johnny and Luther not believe in the efficacy of land mines and bullets, but they chain-smoked. When they sent out messages from the hospital where they were holding hostages, they demanded milk, rice without pork, and cigarettes.

I obsessed about the Htoo twins on the plane. I was anxious about getting back in time to see Malone. He once told me about the bumblebee bat of Thailand which weighed less than a penny. It was the world's smallest mammal. On my fortieth birthday, he had sent me a lifetime membership to The Bat Conservancy and adopted a bat on my behalf. It was a Mexican free-tailed bat, also called a mastiff or bulldog bat, not for any obvious reasons. But Malone took pleasure in the choice. I received an eight-by-ten color photo and an adoption certificate. Had it been any other species, it would have been insufferably cute. Malone wrote:

"Happy Birthday, love—are you feeling terribly old today? Take my word for it, Hon, you're not. I mean, for a plum you're old—even older for a head of lettuce. Still compared to a mountain you have barely begun. But for a woman—you're just right. . . . As you've probably already guessed, I haven't much of anything to say. Then again, I never do. I've been writing a lot lately so I haven't done squat that would be of interest to anyone—living or dead. I haven't been anywhere. I haven't seen anything. . . Face it, dear, I'm a very exciting guy—in comparison to someone in a coma. . . ."

It seemed particularly galling that the flight west took almost an hour longer than the flight east. It had something to do with headwinds and tailwinds. For once I was not sitting next to a fundamentalist Christian or a missionary of any kind. The man next to me managed to sleep the entire trip; he never awoke to eat, he never moved, he never went to the bathroom. Every hour or two I leaned over casually just to make sure he was breathing. Somewhere over the north Atlantic, due south of Cape Farewell, Greenland, I timed the frequency of his breaths because I suspected he was faking sleep in order not to talk to me, because he somehow knew how obsessed I was and that I was looking for any opportunity to expound on my theory that all the wrongs in the world are attributable to religious fundamentalism, because it is fundamentally exclusionary, literal, xenophobic, repressive, and unimaginative. That was and is my belief, and I believed that the man next to me did not want to hear it.

Malone died early the next morning, before I could get up to Maine to see him and say good-bye. He was in terrible pain. In the end it was his heart, congested and unable to support life, that failed. That same afternoon, Aunt Prudence put all his porno videos in a box and had Uncle Basket drive them to the dump. Gus only learned that once we got there, and he was very upset he hadn't made a preemptive strike on Malone's stash. But the magazines still remained unaccounted for, and the teenage nephews were homing in.

Driving north for the memorial service, I read through a pile of ribbon-wrapped letters from Malone. For once, it didn't make me carsick to read while we drove. For years Malone went to Florida in the winter with his parents. They flew south, stayed a week or ten days, and then drove back north. He hated the whole thing.

I hate to travel. I loathe it with every fiber of my being! I detest it with a passion bordering on hysteria! Yet there is another simple truth you must also understand: where my keepers choose to go, I must follow, or

perish in a pool of my own swill. Not what you might term a delightful
prospect, not by any means.

To travel means such unpleasantness as sleeping in a strange bed
where the bumps and cavities of the mattress don't quite conform to my
own bumps and cavities. . . . Have you ever gone through a metal
detector in a wheelchair? I haven't either. What they do is some guy
from Airport Security takes you around to one side and there he gin-
gerly frisks you, all the while looking as if he hopes you don't have any-
thing contagious. It's such a joke. I mean, they never even glance at the
chair or what I'm sitting on. Christ, I could be sitting on enough plas-
tique to blow up three planes. . . .

Once we got there, I was repeatedly told not to call it a
funeral; Christian Scientists do not have funerals. They consider death an insignificant event, and thus they have no
ritual to surround it. But Malone was not a Christian Scientist. I don't know what he called himself, but I know what he
was: a writer, a voyeur, a lover, a pantheist perhaps.

The memorial service was held in a Funeral Home, a
small saltbox house filled with folding chairs and the smell
of disinfectant. There was no music. There were many old
friends of Basket and Prudence, wearing pink Lily dresses or
yacht club blazers and pants held up with belts embroidered
with golf clubs or sailboats. I wore all black, including stockings and underwear, with Malone in mind. I had just reread
the letter where he wrote:

"Were you aware that your mother-in-law has signed you up for a tennis
clinic at the club this summer? She seems to be under the impression that

*you, like she, have an innate love of the sport and that your biggest desire
is to improve your game and become God's gift to the clay court.*

*So, my love. . . . is this one of your burning-most desires? Is your
summer wardrobe going to consist of skimpy little tennis dresses (you
won't hear me complain), brief white shorts and pale pastel polo shirts
with the club burgee embroidered above the left breast?"*

I was sorry not to have worn a black mantilla and a
shorter dress.

The event, which could not even be called a service, was
conducted by a Christian Scientist lay reader who had never
met Malone and insisted on paraphrasing Jesus' speeches and
comparing Malone's fondness for bats to Jesus' exhortation
to the children to come unto Him. I wanted to weep and
gnash my teeth and beat my breast, but I could not. I could
only think of making this lay reader stop speaking, and
never having to hear him again.

Another time, Malone had written:

*"I hate weddings. This ceremony isn't too bad, but you can keep the
reception. There's nothing like a wedding party to make me feel
totally inadequate and socially unacceptable. I mean, I can sit
smack dab in the center of the crowd and if there isn't a member of
the family to keep me company, I may as well be stranded in the
middle of a desert. No one talks to me. No one comes near me. It's
like I have the plague or something; the way everyone sort of avoids
me. This dead zone only the brave dare cross mystically appears
around me in any gathering of more than three. It's a little
depressing, you know."*

The dead zone was in the funeral home. Unlike Malone, I don't hate weddings. And I don't hate to travel. But I hate funerals without music. What can make sense of the pain if not weeping and catharsis? And how better to get there than to sing again the favorite hymns, to choke on tears and struggle through *And did those feet in ancient time Walk upon England's mountains green?* and *A mighty fortress is our God,* and *O God our help in ages?* What makes more sense than to hear *Ave Maria* trumpeted from the choirloft?

Once, years earlier, in the days before the state-of-the-art electric wheelchair, I pushed Malone along a path and we talked about hymns. I told him that *Jerusalem* was my favorite.

"Ah Sweetness," he said. "You've told me that at least ten times."

"Did you know that William Blake wrote it?" I said.

"That, more like a hundred times," Malone said.

"You're not very funny," I said.

"Do you mean funny-haha, or funny-odd, or funny-rowboat?" he said.

"All of the above," I said. "And that line could easily be engraved in stone. So often have we heard it." Touché, I thought.

But Malone knew better. "Right you are, Sweetness, because that is what we do, this family. We tell the same jokes, and pick the same fights. It's the only way we can tell we love each other."

"We can sing the same hymns," I said. "Again and again."

"But do you know my favorite? *Let us with a gladsome mind, Praise the Lord for He is kind,"* he intoned. Malone never could sing.

"Ever faithful, ever sure," I said. "That's awfully cheerful, don't you think?"

"Your friend Milton wrote it," Malone told me.

"I didn't know that."

"I know you didn't. But don't forget. I want you to sing it at my funeral."

"Well I guess that morbidity offsets any cheerfulness lingering in the air," I said.

"Seriously," he said. "Don't forget."

"I won't," I said, and I fully believed that I would not. But I had, until it was too late.

That afternoon, Malone and I had continued down the path, me pushing, Malone offering himself as mosquito bait—at least until the bats came out—towards our houses, our families, our confusion, and our hope.

END

Acknowledgments

I would like to thank my agent, Amy Berkower, for her good sense and great spirit, and my editor, Tina Pohlman, for her vision, her insight, her understanding, and her persistence.

Lis Bensley, Becky Rice, Brad Smith, Lilla Pennant, Harry Stein, Gayle Portnow, Eileen Kitzis, and others read some of the stories in various stages, and I am immensely grateful for their suggestions and encouragement. And I am thankful to Paco Underhill for a hugely helpful introduction.

And as ever, great thanks to Reine and Tristram, and Jeffrey Hewitt, for their patience and kindness and tolerance.